ONLY YOU

Sara Myers

Outskirts Press, Inc.
Denver, Colorado

This is a work of fiction. The events and characters described herein are imaginary and are not intended to refer to specific places or living persons. The opinions expressed in this manuscript are solely the opinions of the author and do not represent the opinions or thoughts of the publisher.

Only You
All Rights Reserved.
Copyright © 2008 Sara Myers
v 2.0

Cover Photo © 2008 JupiterImages Corporation. All rights reserved - used with permission.

This book may not be reproduced, transmitted, or stored in whole or in part by any means, including graphic, electronic, or mechanical without the express written consent of the publisher except in the case of brief quotations embodied in critical articles and reviews.

Outskirts Press, Inc.
http://www.outskirtspress.com

ISBN: 978-1-4327-1800-8

Outskirts Press and the "OP" logo are trademarks belonging to Outskirts Press, Inc.

PRINTED IN THE UNITED STATES OF AMERICA

To the first boy I ever loved
No matter where our lives take us,
I'll always remember the good times.

If You Love Something, Set It Free.
If It Comes Back to You, It is Yours.
If It Doesn't, It Never Was.
-Unknown

Chapter 1

August 2006

The world felt like it was crashing down all around her as she charged out of the school and headed towards her car. Tears burned in her eyes, but she wouldn't let them fall and entertain the students around her by allowing them to see her cry.

A few watched her storm by, and then turned to talk with their friends as if she was invisible. This feeling wasn't new to her. For the past few days she had felt invisible and unimportant.

Someone called her name, but she didn't turn to see who it was. She didn't mean to be rude, but she wasn't in the mood to deal with any sympathy at the moment because she knew she'd break down and sob right there in the middle of the student parking lot.

Her vision was blurry and her heart felt like it was being ripped from her very chest and being squeezed. The sound of squealing tires made her jump and turn to her right. How stupid could she be by walking out in front of a car?

The driver threw up his hands and yelled at her

to watch where she was going.

His harsh words tore at her even more and she didn't even know the dude.

"Krystal. Wait," the voice came again.

Krystal didn't want to turn to her friend. She wanted to get as far away from the school and the memories as she could.

A hand gripped her arm and forced her to stop. Only then did Krystal stop and turn to look into her best friend's scared face. "God, Krystal. You almost got hit. What's wrong?" Sarah asked, noticing Krystal's glassy, red-rimmed, hazel eyes. Just looking into her friend's eyes, Sarah could see her heart being torn into a million pieces. Suddenly the memory of that morning flashed through Sarah's brain and her heart dropped. "Oh, God, Krystal. Did he…?" she started to ask and was surprised when Krystal tried to rip her arm from her grip so she could escape.

"No. I'm not letting you drive in this condition," Sarah said and tightened her hold.

As if a dam had broken, the tears spilled and ran down Krystal's cheeks like a river. Her knees gave out and Sarah had to catch her before she collapsed to the pavement. Krystal had suddenly become a brick of lead and Sarah didn't know how much longer she could hold her friend up.

"Kevin. Get over here and help me," Sarah called and horror filled Krystal's eyes. The tears stopped as abruptly as they had started. "N-no. Let me go. I'm fine."

Only You

"Krystal," Sarah shook her head. "No, you're not. You're a mess."

As her friend's words sank in, the tears came again and before she knew it, Krystal was in Kevin's comforting arms practically being carried over to his truck and her group of friends.

Sarah watched him go, and then looked towards the school. Her heart was pounding in rage and her face was red and heated.

Her vision suddenly zeroed in on him and hatred filled her heart. Taking a deep breath and clenching her fists at her sides, Sarah stormed towards Derek Andrews with angry words burning her tongue.

When Krystal was safe inside her house and everyone was gone, the pain came again.

Sarah had insisted she stay with Krystal, but Krystal wanted to be left alone. She wanted to cry until she fell asleep and didn't want her friends around trying to comfort her.

She had been relieved to find that her mom wasn't home yet and walked slowly to her room.

When she opened the door, his eyes smiled out at her from their frames. She remembered those eyes; those wonderful, golden brown eyes. They were eyes that had lit up with love whenever they landed on her. They were also eyes that had been so kind and concerned when she was having a bad day. The same eyes that had brightened whenever he had laughed or smiled.

Fresh tears spilled from Krystal's eyes as she

remembered looking deep into those eyes and feeling the warmth and love that looked deeply into hers.

Her heart felt like it was being torn all over again so she averted her eyes away from the pictures. She suddenly felt as if she had been punched in the gut when they landed on the promise ring which encircled her left ring finger.

The promises that had been made to her rang in her head as she looked at the little diamond heart.

"I promise to always be there for you when you need me. I promise to love you for the rest of my life no matter what happens. I promise I'll never love another soul because you're my one and only and always will be."

Krystal slipped it from her finger and looked at the engraving on the inside of the band--*My Love*.

A sob escaped Krystal's throat as she flung the ring across the room. She turned towards the pictures and ripped them from the wall. They fell to the floor and the sound of one of them breaking echoed in Krystal's ears, but she didn't care. She was hurt and angry.

With a final sob, she slid to the floor and curled into a ball in the middle of her room and squeezed her eyelids closed. His face loomed there and made her heart lurch with love and hurt.

Crying silently, she replayed that day in her mind....

Why was he avoiding her? What had she done?

Only You

Was he mad at her? Krystal's mind was going crazy along with her body as she waited for the bell to ring. Derek had avoided her that morning when she had gone to meet up with him in between classes and she didn't know why.

For the past few days, he had been different, but she just thought he had a lot on his mind. It was their senior year so the pressure of graduating was not only on; but also the excitement of knowing it was their final year of school.

The bell ringing had her heart hammering. What would he do this time? Would he avoid her again? She didn't know if she'd be able to handle that.

Krystal spotted him down the hall and was tempted to walk away from him like he had done to her. She wanted to let him see how it felt, but her heart and legs wouldn't allow her.

She knew she had a hurt expression on her face as he walked up. The expression on his face was unreadable which really bothered her.

Suddenly, she was walking away from him. She didn't know what made her do it. She just started walking and stopped as soon as his hand gently closed around her arm. Those hands. They had always been kind and gentle with her, but now they felt like the hands of a stranger.

Krystal turned to face him and looked up into the eyes of the boy she had fallen in love with. They looked back at her, but they were empty.

"Why are you avoiding me? What's going on?" she asked. Without answering, he pulled out a folded piece of paper and pressed it into her hands. "No. I don't want it," Krystal said with horror filling her voice.

Derek closed her hand around it. Now, she could see some hurt deep in his eyes, but she looked away because tears of fear and heartbreak were filling her eyes. She didn't have to read the letter to know what was in it. The words seemed to burn through the paper, against her hand, and into her heart.

"There's a reason," he said, in a quiet deep voice.

Not knowing what to do, Krystal pulled her hand from his, and turned, walking quickly to her next class, praying this was all a nightmare.

It was and it was one she couldn't wake up from. Inside the letter, the words glared up at her and sank deep into her heart. He was breaking up with her. She didn't understand why.

He talked about it in the letter, but it was hard to understand in his writing.

Krystal crumbled the paper in her fist and dropped it into her backpack. Ripping a clean sheet from her binder, Krystal went to work writing back begging him to change his mind. She couldn't live without him. Not after the wonderful year and a half they had spent together.

No one would really understand why Krystal was as upset as she was because they didn't understand how perfect Krystal and Derek's relationship had been. The two of them never fought and loved each other with all their hearts.

When Krystal saw him after class, she pressed her note into his hand and turned to walk away before he could say anything. He even had the nerve to ask her if she was okay before she turned. She had wanted to throw her arms around him and press her lips to his, but those days were over. That realization hurt more than anything. She forced her body to turn and walk away from him. He avoided her for the rest of the day. When she tried to talk to him again, he gave her a look as if to say "get lost".

Krystal opened her eyes and sighed heavily. From where she lay she could see one of the pictures and felt her heart fill with love as his eyes beamed out at her. She would love him for the rest of her life even if he didn't feel the same about her.

Chapter 2

June 2007

Students wearing maroon and gray caps and gowns filled the front rows and cheered when the Valedictorian finished her speech.

She beamed as she looked out over Aspen Valley High's graduating class and her classmates who jumped to their feet and were throwing their caps in the air.

Tears clouded her eyes. They were tears of happiness and sadness. The happiness was because she and her friends had finally made it and sadness because she would be losing most of them to colleges throughout the United States.

Sarah was hugging everyone around her. She then turned her eyes to Krystal who stood on stage. She had a mixture of emotions running over her face.

"Hey, get your butt down here," Sarah called up at her and smiled when Krystal looked down at her. Krystal laughed, walked off stage, and was immediately enveloped in hugs from friends.

"Hey, get your hands off my girl," a deep voice

called teasingly. Sarah and the other girls, who had been holding onto Krystal, laughed and stepped back.

Krystal beamed when the tall form of her boyfriend came into view. He looked so good in his gray cap and gown. Still, when she looked him in the eyes, she saw someone else's eyes beaming back at her.

Shaking her head to clear the thought, Krystal rushed into his warm embrace and closed her eyes as she inhaled the scent of his cologne. *Derek.*

This wasn't Derek. This was Jason Gibbons; the boy she had been dating since January. The boy she had gone to winter formal and the prom with. The boy her parents absolutely adored. The boy who had helped her gradually get over the hurt from losing Derek. The boy who would be going to the same college she would be attending. The boy she was in love with.

She stepped back and looked up into Jason's bright blue eyes with a smile.

"That was a wonderful speech, Krys," he said, squeezing her hands. "Thank you. I was shaking the entire time and at one point I thought I was going to forget everything I was going to say," Krystal replied. Jason shook his head. "You did great."

From across the crowd of hugging students, wearing a gray cap and gown like all the other guys, Derek watched as Krystal and her new boyfriend, Jason, kissed and felt his heart drop.

For months he had been beating himself up for losing the only thing that had ever really mattered to him; other than his family.

They had been the whole reason why he had been forced to break up with her and push her away. He had had to take over the business when his father had been called away on other business. He had to become the man of the house. He took up Independent Study to keep up with school so he could graduate.

Now his father was back in charge of the business and the household. Derek had finally turned eighteen and had graduated.

It hadn't been until January, when Derek had come back to school for second semester, that he started to realize what he had lost. By then Krystal had been in the early steps of her new relationship with Jason Gibbons.

Sure, he had seen her date a few other guys, including one of his friends, but he hadn't really cared what she did. He was too stubborn to realize just how much he still loved and wanted her. Whenever he saw her holding hands with a guy or kissing him, he just turned away, feeling nothing. He had even dated two girls during those months after he broke up with her, but neither of them had lasted more than a month. Whenever he had looked at them, he had seen Krystal's face.

He knew it had torn her to pieces to see him with other girls because he had seen it clearly on her face as if she had just written her feelings across her forehead, but he hadn't cared. Now he was paying the price.

Jason Gibbons. Football and track star. Rich family. Adored by parents. Mr. Goody-Goody.

It made him sick to see his Krystal with him. *His Krystal.*

The words flashed through his mind over and over. He remembered a time when he would tell her that she was his and always would be his. Not to be possessive, just to let her know how much he loved her and how much she had meant to him, and still meant to him.

When he looked back towards her, his heart lurched. Her eyes met his from where she stood. For a long time they just stared at each other. He could see the mixture of emotions in her eyes and he knew she could see the same in him. There was love, hurt, anger, maybe a little bit of jealousy. He knew she saw his jealousy when Jason walked up and took her hand.

Her eyes turned away from him and looked up at Jason with love. The same love that she had shown him only months before.

His shoulders slumped. It was too late. He was too late. How could he have been so stupid to throw away something that had meant so much to him and allow her to be snatched up by someone else? Why hadn't he realized that she would probably be snagged by some other guy because of how incredibly amazing she was?

Derek turned away and walked towards the

parking lot. Everyone else was going out to party and enjoy the rest of their graduation. He was going home to lock himself in his room and pull out the pictures he had stashed away in his closet.

Krystal watched Derek walk away and for a split second she debated running after him to offer some friendly words. She didn't, though. The only words that were flashing through her brain were in the form of questions like, "Why did you leave me?" "Why did you hurt me?" "Please stop ignoring me." "Please love me again."

Everything vanished from her mind when he vanished from her view and she felt Jason's hand slip into hers.

"You ready?" he asked.

Krystal looked up at him, and then back to the parking lot where she could see Derek's tail lights driving away. She looked back at Jason with a smile. "Yes."

Why should she be stressing over Derek anyway. She had a brand new boyfriend who was in love with her.

Apart from goodbye parties and Grad night, Krystal was at home packing up her things getting ready to move into her dorm room at UC Davis.

It was the best medical school in California and offered all the classes that Krystal wanted to take to get her ready for her career. She was still stuck between being some sort of a doctor, a psychologist, or a veterinarian and UC Davis offered the classes for all three.

Jason was going to be working towards his medical degree and would be attending UC Davis as well.

Now that she was done with high school, Krystal felt like the summer was flying by and the day when she was due to leave was getting closer and closer. She spent everyday with her family and Jason.

Before she knew it, she was saying goodbye to her family as well as Jason's. She and Jason were in his truck on the road heading north with their stuff in the back, with her car being towed behind.

Davis was a beautiful town. It was green a mostly rural country. The university was even more beautiful with its many buildings and large campus. Krystal couldn't wait to start.

College life was different. There weren't any adults waiting to punish you for your actions or mistakes. Even the professors didn't care whether you showed up to class or not. It was your grade and if you decided to fail and drop out, it didn't take any skin off their noses.

Krystal went to every one of her classes.

Unlike her new friends, who only wanted to party, she wanted to finish college with excellent grades. She wanted to have fun, but she wasn't into partying and getting drunk every night. She even got hired at a nearby Outback restaurant as a hostess.

Between classes, homework, work, spending time with friends and Jason, there wasn't any more room in Krystal's mind to think about anything else; except Derek. She was trying hard to move on and forget about him and the painful memories.

Chapter 3

A baby screamed in his ear as he hurried to bag the lady's groceries. The store was packed with it being Labor Day weekend. Derek was looking forward to going home and relaxing in the new apartment he shared with his two best friends.

Like his friends, he attended classes at Aspen Valley Community College. All his other friends had either gone farther north, south, out of state, or into the military.

He had almost gone off to the military, but in the end, he had decided to stay so he could continue to help his dad. So here he was, working part time at Stater Bros., part time at his father's shop, and attending classes to get an education. Not a day went by that she wasn't on his mind.

He looked over to see the mother cuddling the baby and offering soothing words while the husband paid for the groceries and looked at his wife and baby with pride. His heart warmed when the mom kissed the baby's head. She looked up at her husband, who had turned, with a look filled with love. He remembered that Krystal had given him that look several times every day.

Everything around him stopped as his attention focused fully on the new parents. The dad kissed the baby on the head, and then gently kissed his wife, before turning to push the cart.

Derek snapped back to reality and finished bagging. His heart was hammering now and he could feel sweat beginning to trickle down his back.

The cashier took one look at him and shooed him away. "You go home and relax. You did enough for today."

He waited just to be sure that she was serious, and then walked quickly to his car and got in. He couldn't wait to get home and lay down. The guys had talked about going paintballing or airsofting later, but he wasn't sure if he was in the mood.

As he drove, he thought about Krystal and felt his heart fill with love and regret. He had never stopped loving her even though he had tried his best not to.

Beside him, a silver car drove by. The exact same color, year, and model hers had been.

Feeling his heart lurch, Derek drove after it feeling his heart beginning to hammer against his ribs when he saw the long blonde hair. The driver was wearing sunglasses so he couldn't really see her face, but she was young.

At the next light, he pulled up beside her and looked over. His heart dropped when the girl looked back at him. It wasn't Krystal.

As the light turned green, the girl drove off

while Derek sat staring after her. The blasting of a horn behind him got his attention and with an apologetic wave over his shoulder, he drove on and headed home.

"Isn't this party great?" Krystal's new friend, Devin, yelled over the blasting music.

Krystal looked around at the kids huddled together. She thought it kind of sucked, but she offered her friend a fake smile and nodded.

Honestly, she hadn't really wanted to go out and party, but since it was Labor Day weekend she decided that she needed to get out of her dorm room and away from her books. In a way she was happy with her decision because she knew she would've gotten bored and lonely, but on the other hand, she really wanted to leave and go to sleep.

As she looked around she realized that she was the only person there that she could see that was drinking bottled water. Everyone else had some sort of alcoholic drink in their hand. Krystal shook her head at them and walked over to an empty chair and sat. Her legs and back were killing her. All she wanted to do was go back to her dorm and crawl into bed, but she had to be the designated driver for all her friends.

The party seemed to go on and on into the night. Krystal was relieved when people were starting to leave and stood to find her friends.

After hours of turning down guys and drink offers, she was ready to get the heck out of there. As soon as she found Devin and her other friend, Julie, she grabbed their arms and practically dragged them to her car. She was relieved when they passed out on the way back to the dorms.

While Devin and Julie had hangovers the next morning, Krystal was clear minded and energetic. She ended up leaving the dorm room because all the two girls wanted to do was keep the room dark and sleep.

With no class and no studying, Krystal got in her car and drove into town. She really wanted to spend the day with Jason, but he had class that day and wouldn't be done until later that afternoon. He planned on taking her to dinner that evening.

She walked around the shops and cafes where many college students came to get away from the load of school work. This was the best part of college life. Not having any classes or work to worry about, she could just do whatever she wanted for the entire day.

When she had started walking around, she had sworn to herself that she wouldn't buy anything. But an hour later she was carrying a bag of two new outfits and a new pair of shoes.

At five, Krystal hurried back to the dorm room and was surprised to see Devin and Julie awake and laughing. She was sure they'd sleep all day, and then party all night again.

The girls greeted her and she answered as she

Only You

headed for the bathroom with her outfit for the night. "Ooh, hot date tonight?" Devin asked. Krystal nodded with a smile, shutting the bathroom door before they could say anything else.

She finished putting on her make-up when her cell phone rang.

Both Julie and Devin dove for it and with a victorious smile, Devin answered.

"Hey, Jason. Listen, you want to ditch Krystal and go partying with me and Julie tonight?" Devin asked. Krystal shot into the room and snatched the phone from Devin's hand.

"Hey," she said and gave Devin and Julie a playful glare while they just smiled at her.

Jason was laughing on the other end. "Hey sweetie, you ready?"

"Yep. I'll be down in just a sec," Krystal replied and hung up. She turned to her friends. "Now, you two be good while I'm gone," she said teasingly. Devin and Julie started laughing as Krystal headed for the door.

"No, it's you who should be good…"

Krystal shut the door behind her to block out Devin's words and shook her head with a smile.

Jason took her to a really fancy Italian restaurant called Mama Mia's. When they walked in holding hands, Krystal took one look around and was relieved that she had dressed nicely.

It was about a twenty minute wait for two, but the food was worth the wait and when Krystal and Jason walked from the restaurant, they were both so full they could hardly move.

"Would you like to take a walk and get rid of some of this?" Jason asked as he patted his stomach. Krystal smiled and nodded. Jason took her hand as they started down the walk.

Her pained, shining eyes swam across his from behind his closed lids. He had just watched as a tear escaped and rolled down her cheek and hadn't done or felt anything. He had just turned and walked away leaving her standing in the middle of a crowded hall fighting the tears that he knew were fighting to spill from her eyes. She hadn't chased him to beg him to come back to her or anything. Just stood there and watched him while her heart broke as she accepted the fact that he didn't want anything to do with her.

Derek sat up in bed and covered his face in his hands.

He was glad his roommates had their own rooms so they didn't get to see the tears that rolled down his cheeks.

He couldn't get Krystal off his mind. Every time his mind wandered or his eyes closed, her face was there.

Derek had been dreaming of all the good times he and Krystal had had. Joking around; her sitting in front of him between his outstretched legs with his arms wrapped around her as they watched the sun set. The smell of her hair; the sound of her voice and laugh; the way her eyes had filled with love every time she looked at him. Her smile; the way he felt every time they kissed; movies, track events. The list went on and on. How could he have thrown all that away along with her love as if it had meant nothing to him? How could he have hurt her the way he had when he promised her he would never do something like that to her?

Balling his hands into fists, he looked towards the wall where he had hung up the pictures of her and felt his throat tighten. She stared out at him, all beaming smiles and love-filled eyes. There were even three pictures that had been taken of both of them and the love they felt for each other as they posed for the camera had clearly stood out to the photographer.

Swiping the tears away, Derek turned from the pictures. He laid back down so that he was facing the opposite wall. Next time he saw her, he would talk to her. He would tell her how he felt whether it was really too late or not. At that thought, his eyes turned to his phone. He could always call her.

No. He didn't have her phone number and he felt it was more important to talk to her in person. Could he though?

Derek buried his face in his pillow. What if she wanted nothing to do with him? What if he ran away like a coward again?

Flipping over to his other side, Derek struggled to go back to sleep.

An hour later, he was still on his back staring up at the ceiling.

Several miles north, Krystal was doing the same.

Her date with Jason had been wonderful, but now she was back in her dorm and all alone. The memories had started up as soon as she had laid her head down.

With fists clenched at her sides, she willed herself to sleep.

Her crying over Derek was starting to get ridiculous. He didn't want her. She had moved on with her life just as he had ordered her to do and had probably done the same. Heck, he had probably forgotten all about her and gotten back from a date with a newer, prettier girl. She had a wonderful boyfriend whom she loved a lot; but not as much as she had loved Derek.

Knowing she would just dream about him when and if she even fell asleep, Krystal got out of bed and grabbed her purse and car keys. She needed to drive to get her mind off him.

As she drove around, he still didn't vanish from her mind.

Krystal would be going home in a few weeks to see her family. How would she take being back in her hometown? The same town she knew he was still living in.

Frustrated that even driving wasn't helping, Krystal turned around and headed back to the dorm rooms. Her eyes were getting heavy and all she wanted was a warm bed and, hopefully, a good night's sleep.

Chapter 4

"Go, Cougars" Krystal screamed along with her fifteen year old brother, Brian, and Jason. Her parents sat behind them with a blanket wrapped around their shoulders and cups of hot chocolate in their hands.

It felt good to be back at a high school football game. It felt even better to have Jason sitting beside her and not down on the field being tackled while Krystal sat in the stands watching from between her fingers.

Even though they were college students now, both Krystal and Jason wore their letterman jackets and showed as much school spirit as they had when they were seniors. It had only been a couple months since she had graduated from the school, but it felt like years. Now she was back on a cold October night cheering on her old high school team.

Krystal recognized a lot of people who were at the game and even saw some old friends, who had come down to see their families to get away from college life.

Her mind snapped back to the game when the

buzzer sounded signaling half time. Turning to her parents, Krystal looked at their cups and smiled. "Do you want me to get you some more?" she asked motioning toward the hot chocolate cups. Both nodded, as Krystal's mom handed her some cash.

"You coming?" Krystal asked Brian. He shook his head and pointed towards a group of guys. "I'm going to go hang for a while."

Taking Jason's hand, Krystal left her parents and headed for the snack bar.

"Didn't you want to see the half time show? They're announcing homecoming." Krystal shook her head and shivered a little. "I want to get some of that hot chocolate, too." Jason took off his jacket and wrapped it around her shoulders. She stared up at him with wide eyes. "Aren't you cold?"

He just smiled and plucked at the hooded sweatshirt he had worn underneath his jacket.

"Not right now."

Krystal smiled up at him. She stood on her toes as she gently kissed his lips. She waited for the spark and warm feeling, but like all the other times, it didn't come. Not wanting Jason to see that something was wrong, Krystal turned towards the restrooms. "I'll be right back." She handed him the cash. He squeezed her hand and watched her go.

Derek stood as still as a statue. He didn't even hear what Kevin and Tyler were talking about as he watched Krystal kiss Jason, and then walk towards the restroom. He had seen the look on her face when she pulled back and recognized it instantly. Something had troubled her.

The next thing he saw was another girl walk up to Jason and throw her arms around him. She was probably just an old friend, but as he watched them talk, he started to feel uneasy. She was flirting way too much and from where he stood, Derek could see that Jason was flirting right back.

He recognized the girl as one of the cheerleaders from their graduating class. He looked back towards the restroom. Derek wanted to see her again.

When she walked out, he felt his heart start pounding. She looked different. Not much, but he could definitely tell college had taken her away from a high school teen and turned her into a beautiful young woman. She wore her letterman jacket underneath Jason's jacket. Memories of her wearing his swam through Derek's mind.

Someone punched his arm and forced him to turn his attention away from Krystal and back on his friends.

"Hello. We've been talking to you and oh," Kevin said finally getting the hint when he, too, spotted Krystal. "Well, look who's here," Kevin said and hurried over.

Derek watched as both Tyler and Kevin hurried over and pulled a surprised and excited Krystal into a group hug. He wanted to go over, but his feet seemed glued to the pavement.

For a second, he looked back at Jason to see

what his reaction of two guys grabbing his girl was and frowned when he saw that Jason hadn't even noticed. The girl was whispering something in his ear with a mischievous smile and he was nodding.

Derek turned his eyes back to his friends and Krystal and felt the familiar lurch of his heart. He hadn't felt it since that last day at graduation when his eyes had locked onto Krystal's.

She was looking at him with an unreadable expression while Kevin and Tyler talked excitedly about what had been going on and asking her questions about college life up north.

Derek wanted to be there to hear what she had to say, but he just couldn't find the courage to walk over.

Coward

He remembered his promises to himself to talk to her next time he saw her, but he realized just how hard it was going to be.

Finally, Jason turned around and shook hands with Tyler and Kevin. He then turned to the lady in the snack bar to order the hot chocolates. As soon as he had them, he grabbed Krystal's hand and led her back to the stands.

Realizing they had been dismissed, Kevin and Tyler walked back to Derek. "Man, you should've gone over to say hi. She asked about you." Derek felt his heart soar. "Really? What did she say?" he asked, but the guys just shrugged. "She just asked how you were doing. We told her you were fine and she got kind of quiet. Then her boyfriend dragged her off," Tyler said. "Come on, can we actually watch the rest of the game? I didn't come here to watch parents yell at their children."

Derek laughed and followed his friends. His eyes scanned the crowd for Krystal, but he couldn't find her. He spotted her parents, who held full cups of hot chocolate, and her brother, who was hanging with a group of sophomore boys, but he couldn't find her. He hadn't even talked to her and now he wasn't sure if he'd ever get the chance again.

Krystal was quiet later that night as Jason drove away from the game. She had been surprised when she had seen Derek and had been quiet for the remainder of the game. Jason had seemed distracted so it had given her a chance to think about the way she was feeling.

After kissing Jason, Krystal went to the bathroom to lock herself in a stall to think. She had felt pretty sure of herself and Jason when she walked out of the bathroom, but then she saw Jason flirting with one of the old cheerleaders, been attacked by Kevin and Tyler, and seen Derek. Now she wasn't so sure.

"Who was that girl you were talking to?" she heard herself ask Jason. He didn't seem like the cheating type, but she did know he had a reputation in high school for dating girls for a certain period of time, then moving on. He had confessed this to her on one of their first dates and had sworn to her that he wanted to change that.

She noticed his hands tightened a little on the wheel and in a way it felt as if that pressure was wrapping itself around her heart.

"I knew her from football. She was a cheerleader, remember. I've known her since freshman year. She's just a friend," he assured her and took her hand.

She allowed him to hold it, but she couldn't help but feel uneasy. Thanks to Derek, she felt as if she could no longer trust what guys said to her because she didn't know if they were lying or telling the truth.

Jason walked her to the front door of her parent's home and kissed her gently. Her parents hadn't gotten home yet and Krystal could see what Jason was thinking as he looked down at her. She just squeezed his hands and gave him a weak smile. "I'll see you tomorrow, Jason. I love you."

Disappointment flashed in his eyes but he leaned forward and kissed her once more before stepping back. "I love you, too, Krys." He then walked back to his truck.

Krystal slipped inside and closed the door. She closed her eyes as she rested her forehead against the door and turned the lock. After a minute, she headed to her old room.

Later that night, on the other side of town, a small dark blue truck sat in the drive-way to a house where a certain cheerleader lived.

"Krys honey, I would so love it if you went to

Aspen University. It's hard having you so far away," Krystal's mom said the next afternoon as she and Krystal made dinner. "Davis is only two hours away, mom," Krystal said with a smile.

"I know, but it would be so lovely if I knew you were only a few minutes away," Rebecca Jacobson said with a sigh. Krystal just smiled and shook her head.

"I'm happy at Davis right now. I have friends and great professors."

It was Becky's turn to sigh. "You're right, love. All I care about is that you're happy" Becky replied with a clip of English accent.

Krystal's parents had met when her mom came to the United States from England to be a high school foreign exchange student in her senior year. When she met and fell in love with Jeff Jacobson, she had begged her parents to send her to college in America.

Her mom's parents had come from a long line of wealthy people, so the cost for college in the United States hadn't been a problem, they hadn't wanted to send her for a different reason. Jeff Jacobson.

Jeff's side of the family was far different from the Smyth's side. They hadn't been blue-blooded or rich. Becky fell in love with the Jacobson family while her parents grew to dislike them.

Becky was almost removed from the family, but her father finally came to his senses and told her that he just wanted her to be happy.

"How is Jason doing? He's coming tonight, right?" Becky asked as she prepared a salad. In an hour, friends and family would be showing up for a famous Jacobson barbeque.

Krystal smiled, "yeah, he'll be kind of late, but he'll be here. He can't wait to see everyone again."

Becky smiled, "everyone can't wait to see him again. They can't wait to see you either."

Chapter 5

An hour later, the house was filled with the sound of laughter and squeals of delight as Krystal was pulled into hug after hug from her family and friends, whom she considered family.

Once the excitement had died down, the men headed outside to drink beers and talk about women and whatever else guys liked to talk about while the women stayed inside and talked about the men and girl stuff.

Krystal had missed this terribly. She could remember sitting at the table when she was younger and feeling older because she had been included in grown up talk. Sure, there had been several times when she was told to cover her ears or leave the room for a minute, but other than that she had felt as if she was truly apart of the conversation even if she hadn't understood some of the things that were talked about.

Now, being eighteen, she was allowed to listen to the entire conversation and had the pleasure of seeing her mom turn red in embarrassment when one of the women said something that she normally wouldn't have been allowed to hear when she was younger.

Chips and other snacks were passed around and carbs were forgotten as plates were filled.

Outside, Krystal could hear the younger kids running around playing a game of tag despite the cold weather and smiled as she listened to their high pitched giggles and squeals.

In the living room, Brian sat watching TV with his current girlfriend and another one of his friends whom he had invited over. Krystal had been filled in on all the gossip about Brian and Jessie. They had been dating only two weeks, but Krystal's mom had already caught them kissing and said that Jessie was always over watching movies with Brian.

"Speaking of girlfriends and boyfriends. Where is that handsome young man you've been dating?" Becky's best friend, Brianne, asked. "He should be here soon" Krystal said and smiled. Brianne leaned back in her seat and turned to the other women.

"Oh. Just the other day I saw that other young man. What was his name? Derek. That's right, Derek" she said and Krystal's spine stiffened. "He was bagging groceries in Stater Bros. and doing a fine job too. I said hi, but he must not have heard me" Brianne said and looked back at Krystal. "It's a shame you too split up. He was a nice young man too."

"He probably did hear you, but he ignored you. He wasn't the boy I thought he was" Krystal said icily. Brianne's eyebrows raised as she smiled. "No worries. You're with a nice young man now."

Only You

Krystal smiled thinking of Jason and glanced at the clock. Where was he?

"I really need to go. My girlfriend is expecting me" Jason said and walked towards the door. He stopped when Brittany's hand grabbed his arm and yanked him back so she could press her lips against his. "Aw, come on. She can wait" Brittany said with a purr to her voice as she kissed Jason's neck. His hands trembled. Brittany smiled to herself. Krystal Jacobson was no threat to her.

Jason reluctantly stepped back and shook his head.

"I don't want to make her suspicious. She probably already is with me being so late" Jason said and turned to the door. Brittany pulled him around again and smiled up at him, "let her get suspicious" she whispered and kissed him again.

Jason pulled himself away and walked out the door to his truck. Behind him, Brittany stood in the open doorway wearing his hooded sweatshirt and smiling dreamily as she watched him go. Just before he drove off, he stuck his head out the window.

"I'll try to come back by before I leave." With that he waved and drove away.

Brittany waved until he disappeared, then smiled, this time in victory. Krystal was so done for.

Everyone jumped to their feet and rushed forward to hug Jason when he walked through the door. Seeing their excitement and Krystal's lovely smile stabbed Jason with guilt, but he waved the feeling away and stepped forward to kiss her.

That's when the perfume floated through the air and made Krystal's eyes and senses burn.

Jason felt her tense under his hands and was surprised when she shoved him back. The women around them froze and their eyes widened. The men came in and stopped as well, then hurried back outside when they sensed the tension. Brian, Jessie, and Brian's friend hurried outside to watch the kids.

Krystal grabbed Jason's shirt and sniffed it. There it was. She remembered smelling it the night before when that cheerleader, Brittany, had been standing nearby.

"I can explain, Krys" Jason said and felt like hitting himself in the forehead. How was he going to explain that he had cheated on her?

"Don't. Just….don't" Krystal said and could feel her heart ripping all over again as the realization sank in.

Jason reached out for her and knew it was a useless movement because Krystal just slapped it away.

She was too shocked, hurt, and angry to say anything and the silence was making everyone feel awkward.

Becky shooed the women from the living room sensing her daughter needed to deal with this without having an audience.

"Krystal, I…" Jason couldn't find the words. "Cheated on me" Krystal finished for him. He could hear the ice in her voice, then the breaking of it.

He remained silent. How could he lie. It was the truth. His shoulders slumped as she looked up at him. Her eyes were amazingly hard and clear of tears.

"It was Brittany wasn't it?" she asked and he slowly nodded.

"Why?" she screamed. The sudden volume made him jump out of his skin. The house went dead silent as she stood and glared at him. Now the tears were coming. Knowing that he had broken her, broke his heart and he suddenly hated himself for being so stupid.

"I-I don't know" he whispered. Krystal stepped forward and shoved him. "You don't know? You don't know why you went behind my back and cheated on me with Brittany?" she shrieked in anger and hurt.

Now he could feel anger and he had no clue why. He really had no reason to be angry, it was her who had the right to be angry.

Suddenly the words were out of his mouth and he couldn't snatch them back. "You wouldn't go any farther and I was tired of waiting. Brittany would."

All color drained from Krystal's face and a single, shocked tear rolled down her cheek and fell to the floor. Before she could say anything, her dad was standing between her and Jason and glaring daggers at him. "You have two seconds to get out of my house and as far away from my family as you possibly can" he said so calmly and quietly. It was scary and Jason was more than happy to get out of there. The whole family had suddenly appeared and were glaring at him. He could see the extreme disappointment on their faces and the anger. He looked at Krystal and saw that she wasn't even looking at him. She was standing as still as a statue staring at the floor. Anger replaced guilt as he turned and stormed from the house. He wanted to slam the door, but didn't because then he could possibly break something and have to pay for it.

Jeff turned to his daughter. "Your mother and I would prefer you go to college closer to home. I don't want you anywhere near that…" he didn't even finish because there were young children present.

Krystal didn't look at him, but she slowly nodded and headed for her room.

A few minutes later, all the women huddled in Krystal's room offering comforting words while Becky rocked her sobbing daughter.

"He's scum …. no good …. he doesn't deserve you" was repeated, but Krystal didn't hear it as she buried her face in her mom's shirt and felt her heart being torn to pieces all over again.

Chapter 6

December 2010

Derek smiled as Ashley Peters walked up to him, threw her arms around his neck, and pressed her lips gently to his. They had been together since September when he had helped her carry her groceries to her car. They had been attracted to each other almost instantly and at the end of their first date, had nervously kissed each other good night.

Derek had felt sparks and he didn't see Krystal's face when he looked at Ashley, which told him he was finally getting over Krystal. Part of him hated to let her go, but he also knew she was getting on with her life and had probably let him go ages ago. It had been three years since he had seen or heard of her. He and Ashley had a lot in common and before long he realized he was starting to fall in love with her, which honestly scared the crap out of him.

At first he hadn't been ready to give his heart to another woman. It had taken two and a half years to stop thinking about Krystal so much. He had dated on and off, but none of them had compared to what he and Krystal had once shared. Not until Ashley.

As he held her closely and breathed in the smell of her perfume he couldn't help but think about Krystal. He had heard that she had dropped out of Davis and had started taking classes at Aspen University, but he hadn't seen her around. Since Aspen Valley was so small, this had surprised him. Another thing about Aspen Valley being so small was how fast word had traveled about Krystal and Jason.

Derek had been shocked when he overheard some people gossiping about it in the grocery store. He never could've pictured Jason, perfect Jason, cheating on someone. For a while he had debated whether or not he should call and see how Krystal was doing, but in the end he had decided it was best for her not to have to see the first boy who broke her heart.

Ashley stepped back and took his hands. "Do you know what today is?" she asked with a grin. He grinned right back. Of course he did. He had always been good about keeping track of special dates.

"Our three month anniversary and our date at Chili's" he replied and she beamed.

A date at Chili's didn't seem so romantic for an occasion like an anniversary, but both he and Ashley loved that restaurant and went to dinner there every time they went out.

Ashley stood on her toes and kissed him, then took his hand. Their fingers laced as they headed down the walk.

People sitting outside the coffee shop or walking down the sidewalk turned to watch them pass. Some smiled, but others just shook their heads. Derek knew a lot of people had been disappointed when he and Krystal had broken up. They had been the cutest, most popular couple in town. *Get over it already, I am*, he thought as he shook his own head, but he couldn't help but wonder, *am I really*.

Krystal massaged her temples with her fingers as she sat in the back room at Chili's. It was packed that night just like it was almost every night and all the noises and demands were giving her a headache. Chili's was the most popular restaurant in Aspen Valley. She had been working there ever since she started classes at AVU after her break up with Jason.

She had moved back in with her parents, but was working towards getting her own apartment once she found one or two friends to share the expenses with.

Her parents loved having her in the house, but with Brian now off at college somewhere in southern California, they were ready to retire and go on with their lives without having their twenty-one year old daughter still living with them.

She had lost count of how many times they had told her she was old enough to be out on her own and starting her life. They hadn't been mean about it, but she could tell they were done with having children in the house.

Taking a deep breath, Krystal stood and headed

to the kitchen where orders were waiting. She piled the meals on a big round plate and carried it all out on one arm to the hungry customers.

The night shift at Chili's seemed endless. Even with the short break she had just finished.

Single men flirted, married, drunk men flirted, drinks were continuously being filled, and questions like "how is everything" and "can I get you anything else" were continuously asked.

There were good tips and there were bad tips.

Thankfully, Krystal had never been complained about. Most of the other waitresses were jealous of her because people were always giving her good tips and complimenting her service while they were complained about and received not so good tips.

As Krystal hurried back into the kitchen to retrieve some dipping sauce, she almost ran right into one of the bus boys. He stepped to the side and smiled down at her which made her cheeks turn pink. "Watch where you're going there, Krystal" he said jokingly. "Sorry, Josh" she replied and walked around him.

She could feel his eyes on the back of her neck and felt her neck and face heat at the thought of his striking, steel gray eyes, and ruffled blonde hair. Shaking her head, she asked for a cup of ranch dressing, then hurried back out into the noisy restaurant.

A half and hour later, Derek and Ashley walked in hand in hand and gave the hostess their name.

Only You

Allie looked at Derek for a while, then looked down at her list as she jotted down his name. "It'll be about fifteen minutes" she told them. Derek smiled and nodded, then led Ashley over to some cushioned seats.

Allie watched them out of the corner of her eye and tried to figure out why Derek looked so familiar. She stared at his name for what seemed like ten minutes before it finally clicked and her heart started hammering. Derek Andrews. She looked at him with wide eyes. He had changed. He was older, taller, and more manly. Even though he looked so great, she couldn't help but still feel a little angry towards him. She could still remember that day when he broke up with Krystal and left her standing there with her heart tearing. She had been one of Krystal's good friends and still was. In fact, she was Krystal's new best friend and future roommate once she and Krystal found a nice apartment and someone else to share it with.

Allie looked around the restaurant and spotted Krystal taking some empty plates back to the kitchen. Derek and Ashley would be sitting in her section. *Surprise, Krys.*

When Derek's name was called, Allie led him and Ashley towards one of the smaller booths. They sat and she handed them menus and silverware. "Krystal will be your waitress tonight. Enjoy" Allie said and saw Derek's surprise before she walked away.

He stared after Allie. He had recognized her

when they walked in, but hadn't wanted to say anything to her and bring up the past. He looked around the restaurant. *Krystal will be your waitress tonight...* His heart started to pound as he looked back at Ashley.

She was too focused on reading the menu to notice his sudden discomfort which he was relieved for. He tried to relax, but his eyes kept scanning the restaurant.

Krystal stopped by Allie's hostess stand to get two more place settings and a children's menu and noticed how her friend was distracted. "What's up?" she asked. Allie jumped and turned to her. "Nothing. Oh, you have table 13" Allie replied. Krystal nodded and headed that way. She stopped in her tracks when she recognized the back of the guy's head. She knew that figure too well. Her heart plummeted at the sight of the girl that sat facing her.

She wanted to walk away and give the table to one of the other waitresses, but she'd get in trouble if she did.

She carried the place settings and the children's menu to her bigger party, then took a deep breath and pulled out her notepad. Every time she lifted her feet, it felt like she had lead in her shoes. Keeping her eyes on her notepad, she stepped up to the table. "What can I get you to drink?" she asked.

Her heart was hammering so loud in her ears, she didn't think she'd be able to hear what they said.

Only You

The girl spoke right up without even looking at her. "I'll have a diet coke." Krystal didn't think she needed to be having anything that was diet, but she jotted it down and painfully turned her eyes to Derek.

He was staring up at her with a mixture of emotions running over his face. She glared back at him, deliberating turning her eyes hard and cold.

God he was so HOT. He had grown a lot since she had seen him three years ago at the football game. His dark brown hair was the same length as it had always been and those golden brown eyes were exactly the same. It was hard for her to be hard towards him, but he had broken her heart once and she didn't know if she could ever forgive him no matter how much she still loved him.

"Derek" Ashley said and noticed the look the two of them were exchanging. It made her uneasy. "Derek" she repeated a little more firmly. It got his attention and he dropped his eyes to his menu while his heart pounded in his ears. "Iced tea" he said. He didn't know it, but Krystal had already written his drink down.

As she hurried away, the drift of air left in her wake floated to his nostrils. As if a lock had been broken, the doors to his mind flew open and memories spilled out at the smell of her perfume. He closed his eyes and willed himself to calm down, but her eyes were once again glaring at him from behind his lids.

This time they had been filled with hurt. He had

seen her trying to keep her real feelings hidden behind a hard look, but the hurt she felt had been clear.

She was so different, but in a good way. She now had the look of a beautiful young woman and her hair had been styled a different way. Her eyes were the same, but her face had changed thanks to everything she had gone through. Sighing, Derek looked down at the menu and was relieved when Ashley broke the silence between them and started talking. He tried to listen, but his mind kept wandering.

"Okay. Who was that girl? Should I be worried?" she asked. She wasn't stupid. She could see that his mind was elsewhere. His eyes snapped back to hers and widened a little. "No. Of course not. I won't lie to you, she was my sweetheart back in high school until I broke up with her in the beginning of our senior year. I didn't end it well. I'm over her though so don't worry" he said. Okay, so he had lied about saying he was over Krystal.

Ashley smiled as he took her hand and kissed it, "okay, then I won't worry anymore" she said and leaned across the table to kiss him, making sure Krystal got a full view of it when she carried their drinks to the table.

Krystal wanted to drop the drinks and run when Ashley kissed Derek right in front of her, but instead she stiffened her spine and set the drinks down on the coasters, then pulled out her notepad.

"Would you like some appetizers?"

An hour later, Krystal collected the bill and tip Derek had left on the table. Tears were forming in her eyes, but she blinked them back as Josh walked over to clear the table.

"Old boyfriend?"

Krystal whipped around and stared at him. He shrugged and smiled. She sighed and nodded. While he washed and dried the table, she told him what had happened so many years ago and was surprised when he pulled her into a one-armed hug. "Ah, don't worry about it. He's a jerk. He never deserved you" Josh said and walked away.

Krystal watched him, then smiled as she headed back to the kitchen.

Chapter 7

"It's perfect" Krystal cried as she and Allie did a little dance, then raced to the front door of their new apartment. Their third roommate followed slowly with his hands tucked in his pockets. He was excited, but his pride kept him from doing a dance like the girls had.

Krystal looked back at him and held out her hand.

"Come on, Josh."

He smiled and took her hand as she led him inside. The moving van would be arriving shortly with the small amount of furniture and boxes they had.

The apartment was newer than the others throughout town. It was two storied with three small rooms and two small bathrooms, one downstairs and one upstairs.

The girls had already claimed the one upstairs since they were sharing the one that one was larger and had two sinks plus a shower/bath. The downstairs bathroom was smaller with one sink, a toilet, and a shower.

Josh had been thrilled when Allie asked him to

be their third roommate. Just a week ago, his parents had thrown him out of their house when he and his dad got into an argument, and he had been staying at his buddy's place. He had been grateful when his friend took him in, but after a while he realized it just wasn't working out.

Josh looked around the apartment as Krystal let go of his hand and walked over to open some of the windows and let in the warm April breeze. The two of them had been seeing each other for the past month.

When the van arrived, the girls hurried out to start carrying in boxes while Josh helped carry in the furniture. The three of them had pitched in to buy their own furniture, though some of it had been donated by Krystal and Allie's parents.

For the remainder of the afternoon, the three of them arranged the furniture, fought over which rooms they wanted, then unpacked their boxes.

Josh had taken the bedroom that was downstairs near the bathroom and had allowed the girls to fight over the two upstairs.

He smiled as he listened to them and began to wonder if he had made a mistake moving in with two girls when he was the only guy. Josh just shrugged and ripped open the next box.

"How are you and Ashley doing?" Tyler asked as he and Derek sat in the nearest bar/restaurant, Mike's. Derek had never been a drinker and held a bottle of water while Tyler held a beer. Besides, he had to be the designated driver. He shrugged, "she was really grumpy today and told me she needed to be alone so I'm leaving her alone" Derek grumbled. "Women" Tyler muttered and Derek smiled.

"What happened with that brunette you were seeing?" Derek asked. Tyler shrugged, "she grew bored and went off with some married lawyer from New York." Derek shook his head.

"Hey, there's some girls who are checking you out. Go ask them to dance" Tyler said and elbowed Derek in the ribs. Out of curiosity, Derek turned to look. In the back of his mind he wondered if one of them was Krystal. None of them were, but they were checking him out. He turned back around, not want to make them think he was interested. "I have a girlfriend, Ty" he said. Tyler shrugged and set his beer down, "snooze you lose."

Derek shook his head as Tyler wandered over to the girls, then took another sip of his water and looked around at the other men and women who sat at the bar. There was no way he'd see Krystal in here. This wasn't her kind of atmosphere. It wasn't his either, but he didn't want Tyler driving home after drinking and possibly getting into an accident or being taken to jail.

"You sure you don't want anything, baby doll?" the lady working behind the bar asked and leaned over, fluttering her eyelashes. He looked up and shook his head, then turned away. His heart jumped when Krystal walked through the door followed by Allie and some tall guy.

Only You

Krystal couldn't believe Allie had dragged her here, but the thought of dancing and having a good time had sounded good after a long day of working around the apartment.

Allie headed straight for the bar, then turned, "you guys want anything?" she called over the music. Krystal shook her head, but Josh followed Allie over.

Shrugging, Krystal grabbed a table and sat down. Her foot tapped along with the country song which blasted through the speakers and for a while she watched some big biker men play a game of pool. The dance floor was crowded and Krystal giggled as she watched the ones, who had had to much to drink, sway and almost fall over. It wasn't all that funny, but then Krystal thought it was stupid for people to go and get themselves drunk.

Josh and Allie came back to the table and sat down. Both carried glasses of some colorful alcoholic drink, then Allie handed Krystal a glass of water. "I promise, it's just water" Allie said when Krystal eyed it suspiciously. "I also ordered some fries so those should be here any minute."

The thought of warm French fries had Krystal's stomach growling and her mouth watering. She hadn't eaten much all day and was starving. She could feel someone watching her, but from where she sat, she couldn't see the part of the bar where Derek sat. Still, she looked around and smiled when she spotted Tyler on the dance floor dancing with three women who looked to be in their early thirties.

"I'll be right back" she told Allie and Josh, then stood and made her way onto the dance floor.

Tyler let out a whoop when he saw her walking towards him and hurried towards her to lift her off the ground in a crushing bear hug. Krystal laughed as he swung her around in a circle before setting her on her feet, then stepping back and resting his hands on her shoulders.

"Wow" was all he could say as he studied the young woman whom he had known since middle school.

"It's good to see you too, Ty. I thought you'd be out of Aspen Valley by now."

"Not yet. I still have to finish up this year of college, then I'll figure out where I want to go" he replied. "Oh. That's right. I forgot you were aiming towards your Bachelor's degree and not just your Associates. What are you planning to be?" she asked and he shrugged. "I'll probably be going into construction. What about you? Wow!" he said and Krystal laughed.

"I've decided I'm going to be a psychologist" she yelled over the music. His eyes widened as he smiled. "That's great, Krys. Hey, Allie" he cried and threw his arms around her. Allie was beaming and her eyes were bright with happy tears as she held him close. "Hey, Ty. I've missed you" she yelled back when she stepped back to look up at him. She and Tyler had been a couple back in their sophomore and junior year and had split up when they realized their relationship as a couple was starting to go downhill.

It had been hard for both, but they had gone back to being good friends.

"God, I've missed you too, Allie" he replied and hugged her again.

His face went back to being a little serious when Josh walked up. "Oh Ty, this is our friend, Josh" Allie said, then smiled at Krystal, "well, he's my friend. He and Krystal have been seeing each other for the past month" she added and both Krystal and Josh's cheeks went pink. Tyler held out his hand and Josh shook it.

"Nice to meet you."

Tyler turned back to Krystal, this time his eyes were wide. "Oh. Guess who else is here?" he asked and grinned. Krystal's eyes widened in horror as she followed Tyler's eyes and locked eyes with Derek who looked just as shocked as she did. She turned away and took Josh's hand, "you want to dance?" she asked and pulled Josh into the crowd of dancing people.

Tyler shrugged at Derek, then took Allie's hand and followed Krystal and Josh.

Derek tried to spot Krystal in the group of people and saw her dancing with the tall blonde he had seen shake Tyler's hand. He wanted to leave, but he knew he couldn't leave Tyler. Anger flared in his chest when he thought about the way Krystal had looked at him. He had been too far away to read her expressions, but he could tell she had been shocked to see him there sitting at the bar. He really needed to talk to her, but he wasn't sure if he could with that guy hanging around her.

He got to his feet and clenching his fists, walked into the dancing crowd towards her. She jumped when he took her arm. He looked at the guy she was dancing with, then back at her. "I need to talk to you" he yelled over the music.

He could see the flame in her gaze. "I'm dancing" she yelled back.

"Please."

The guy rested a hand on her shoulder and sent Derek a warning glare.

"Please. I just need to talk to her for a sec, then you guys can go back to dancing" he said.

Krystal sent Josh a look, then pulled her arm from Derek's grip and walked towards the back door. Derek hurried after her, amazed at her speed.

Once outside, she stopped and crossed her arms across her chest, but kept her back to him.

"What do you want?" she asked. Now that it was quieter, she said it so quietly, he almost didn't hear what she had said. Suddenly he realized he hadn't really thought of what he wanted to say and for a while they stood in awkward silence.

A breeze picked up and ruffled Krystal's hair. Hair that Derek had run his fingers through a dozen times. Hair that had always smelled so good to him.

Sighing, he shoved his hands in his pockets and said the first thing that came to mind.

"I'm so sorry, Krystal. For everything."

He jumped backwards when she spun around and

launched herself at him, grabbing his shirt and pushing him back. Now he could see the tears and the anger in her eyes.

"You're too late" she cried and rushed back into the bar. He chased after her and cursed when he lost her. When he found Tyler, he hurried over.

"Did you see Krystal?"

"Yeah, she and her boyfriend just left. You don't mind taking Allie home when we leave do you?" he asked. Derek's shoulder slumped as he shook his head.

"Can we go. I want to get out of here?"

Tyler looked hard at his friend and nodded. "Sure. I'm getting tired anyway" he replied and took Allie's hand.

When Derek pulled up in front of Allie's apartment, he stayed in the car as Tyler walked Allie to the door. He knew Krystal was inside, but for some reason, he couldn't get himself to get out and try to talk to her. He had screwed up. Krystal was right. He was too late and he doubted anything could change that.

Josh stood outside Krystal's door when Allie came upstairs and looked at her with a worried expression. "She's been sobbing ever since we got home and she won't let me in to comfort her" he said. Allie shooed him away. "She's dealt with enough men tonight. Go on. I'll handle this" Allie said and knocked on the door. Even she was told to go away. Sighing, Allie looked back at Josh and shrugged. "Leave her alone."

Inside her room, Krystal kept her face buried in her pillows as the tears spilled from her eyes. Pictures of Derek lay in pieces around her bed.

Krystal was fully recovered the following day and went shopping with Allie while Josh went out to hang with some old friends. The three of them wanted to hold a party in their new apartment, but first they wanted to liven it up with things like pictures, house plants, and other house décor.

"So. What happened last night with Derek?" Allie asked as she and Krystal studied everything in the kitchen section of the store Bed, Bath, and Beyond.

Krystal shrugged. "He just said he was sorry for everything. I pushed him away and told him he was too late. I didn't let him say anything else" she replied. Allie shrugged. "I think he's finally regretting what he did to you. He doesn't deserve you, Krystal. Not after what he did to you" she said and Krystal nodded. "I know that now. What do you think of this?" she asked and held up a hammock looking thing for bananas. "Ooh. Very cute" Allie said and put it in the cart.

Josh thought the things the girls bought were too feminine so he was relieved when they showed him some things that were more masculine. "We thought of you, Josh. How could we forget we have a man for a roommate" Allie said with a smile.

Things weren't going too well for Derek across town. Once again, Ashley was in a sour mood and was frustrating him even more. He tried to remain calm, but before long he, too, was in a bad mood and argued right back with her.

"Get out. Just get out!" she yelled, and pushed him towards the front door. It had been the second time in less than twenty four hours that he had been pushed away.

Without saying anything, Derek walked from Ashley's house and got into his car. Taking a deep breath, he drove away suddenly looking forward to the day when he graduated from AVU with his Bachelor's degree and could finally leave this horrible town.

Of course Ashley called later that night and apologized to him over and over on his answering machine, but he was being stubborn and didn't pick up or call her back. Tyler just raised his eyebrows at Derek.

"What?" Derek snapped. Tyler raised his hands as if in defense, "nothing, sorry man. I'll see you later. I have a date with Allie tonight," he said and hurried from the house.

Kevin was sprawled out on the couch in his boxers and a white t-shirt watching TV and didn't bother Derek in fear that he, too, would be snapped at.

Sighing, Derek headed to his room to work on some homework and study for a test he had the next day.

Chapter 8

"And where are you going?" Krystal asked with a smile as she leaned against the door jam. Allie was styling her hair and was all dressed up like she was going out. "I have a date with Tyler tonight. He asked me last night at Mike's" Allie replied and smiled excitedly. "He should be here any minute" she added a little nervously. Krystal smiled.

As Allie passed her on the way downstairs, she sent Krystal a smile over her shoulder. "I'm not sure when I'll be back so you'll be alone with Josh for a while. Watch some movies or something" Allie said and Krystal shrugged. "I guess we will once he gets back from work" Krystal replied just as the doorbell rang.

Allie gave a little squeal of delight and threw open the front door. Krystal was able to greet Tyler before Allie practically dragged him to his car.

Krystal smiled as she watched them drive away. It was good to see Allie and Tyler back together. She remembered when the two of them had broken up and remembered how upset she had been. Allie and Tyler had made a perfect couple. They still did.

Krystal stepped back into the house and closed the door. The house was dead silent and suddenly lonely. Sighing, Krystal picked a DVD, grabbed some snacks, and started to watch the movie.

Krystal's mind started to wander and soon it was traveling down memory lane. She remembered all the times Derek had taken her to the movies, then dinner after. Even though no one was around, Krystal blushed a little when she thought about how they had sat in his car after dinner and made out like typical love-struck teenagers.

She closed her eyes and sighed as his face swam through her mind. Just last night, she had seen the love, hurt, and regret in his eyes when he looked at her and it had scared her. She hadn't known how to react and honestly still didn't even though she had gone over the possible future conversation over and over in her head during the months after their break-up. She had come up with things he might say to her and think of how to reply, but whenever she had the chance to say those things to his face, she turned into the chicken she had always been and remained quiet.

Krystal had never been open about her feelings. She knew it had frustrated Derek when he spilled his heart out to her and she did nothing, but it had always been because she knew he'd get his feelings hurt or get angry and she hadn't wanted to go there and possibly lose him. It was all thanks to her dad who had always thrown a fit when she finally told him what was on her mind after he continuously demanded she tell him.

Derek had told her that he wasn't like her dad and that she could always tell him what was on her mind, but when she did, his feelings ended up getting hurt and he turned distant. Krystal had hated feeling like crap when that happened and it had been hard to get Derek back to his usual self. Now she regretted it and was trying to fix that part about her.

There had been so many things she had wanted to tell him the night before, but something had stopped her and made her run from him.

Krystal was surprised when she woke up an hour later. The house was dark and the TV was turned off and when Krystal went to shift she realized a blanket had been draped over her. Smiling, she pushed it off and tip-toed to Josh's room.

The door was open and with the moonlight streaming in through his window, she could see him laying on his bed fast asleep. She tip-toed away from his door and up the stairs.

Allie wasn't back yet so Krystal headed into her room and changed into the tank top and baggy plaid pants she wore to bed, then slipped into bed and fell into a deep, dreamless sleep.

Cheers erupted as students stood and threw their caps into the air. This time Krystal was among them and watched as her cap sailed through the air under the hot June sun. She had finally completed her first four years of college and had gotten her Bachelor's degree in animal science. She still had four more years to get her Master's, but it sure felt good to know she had completed the first four with great grades.

Of course there were parties she and Allie had been invited to since a lot of their friends were done with college and going off to start their own jobs or get married and start families.

As Krystal stood and looked around at the students around her, she felt a pang of sadness. It was just like high school. So many of her new friends were leaving. Even Derek.

Krystal had sworn she wouldn't get all upset when Allie gave her the news that Derek would be heading back to the town he had grown up in as a child, but she was. His parents had moved back there when he graduated from high school and he would be continuing to work with his dad.

She looked over to where Derek stood and had a flashback of when she looked at him during their high school graduation. He didn't meet her eyes this time, but she knew he could feel her watching him and when she turned her gaze away, she could feel him turn to look at her. *Goodbye Derek*, she thought and smiled when Allie pulled her into a group hug with three of her other friends.

Knowing it was the last time he could have fun and hang with his friends before leaving, Derek went to the party later that night. He knew Krystal would be there so he'd make sure he avoided her. It wouldn't be that hard after he avoided her for four and a half years.

The house was packed with graduating college students from ages 21 and up and music blasted through the speakers. The air was thick with smoke and made Derek's eyes sting as he worked his way through the large crowds of people.

Couples sat on the couches or stood in a corner and made out while others slipped upstairs with mischievous smiles on their faces.

Derek finally found Tyler and Kevin and smiled when he saw Tyler's arm draped around Allie's shoulder. "So, you two finally hooked up again?" he said and Allie beamed as she and Tyler nodded. Derek turned to Kevin, "weren't you bringing, Hilary?"

Kevin shook his head, "I broke up with her earlier today" he replied and shrugged his shoulders. "That's too bad. What happened?" Derek asked.

"It just wasn't working out between us."

"That's been happening a lot lately" Allie said and turned to Tyler since she knew Derek wouldn't care, "just a few days ago, Josh and Krystal split up. It just wasn't working for either of them. Josh had feelings for another girl and Krystal just wasn't comfortable in the relationship. She's been that way lately. Can't say I blame her. After what she went through when the relationships that meant a lot to her ended" Allie said and glared at Derek.

Derek just dropped his eyes. He wanted to walk

away, but he didn't know where else to go or who else to talk to.

"Where is Krystal? I haven't seen her since graduation today" Derek heard Tyler ask. "She decided she didn't want to come. She wanted to go home and see her family. I guess her brother, Brian, finally came to visit and he was bringing his new girlfriend" Allie replied. "She already said goodbye to everyone whose leaving. Oh Ty, you're invited to our end of the year party. Our apartment is finally finished and ready for a party" Allie said.

Tyler laughed, "what so it can be trashed again?" he asked and Allie smiled, "we're keeping it small. Just really good friends" she replied.

Like Tyler and Derek, Allie had finished college, but she was going to keep living with Krystal and working at Chili's until she figured out what she wanted to do with her life. She didn't want to stay in Aspen Valley for the rest of her life, but she didn't know where else to go at the moment.

"When is it?" Tyler asked as he slipped an arm around Allie's shoulders. "Next weekend. It starts at seven and goes until everyone's gone" Allie replied. Not wanting to be rude, she turned to Kevin and Derek, "you guys can come too if you want" she said, but mostly looked at Kevin. Derek knew she was just being nice, but he knew she really wanted him to stay as far away from Krystal as possible. Kevin smiled, "I'll definitely be there."

While Allie, Tyler, Kevin, and Derek stood

around talking about the upcoming party, Krystal sat in her parent's dining room across from Brian's new girlfriend and her possible sister-in-law, Amanda. All through dinner, Amanda had been questioned by Krystal's parents and Krystal had enjoyed listening to the girl's answers. Like her parents, Krystal was protective of her little brother and didn't want him dating some cheap girl.

She had been surprised by Amanda's replies. Amanda came from a family where everyone had some kind of medical career. She was studying to become a surgeon and had excellent grades.

By the end of the night, Krystal's parents adored Amanda and Krystal figured she wouldn't mind having Amanda for a sister-in-law.

As Krystal helped her mom wash the dishes, she looked out at her brother and Amanda, who sat cuddled outside on the porch swing, and felt a pang of jealousy. She remembered a time when she and Derek had sat on the swing with his arms wrapped around her and her head resting on his shoulder as they watched the sun set or looked up at the stars. Krystal turned away and closed her eyes as she dried the dish with a towel

"Derek was at the party last night" Allie said the next morning as she poured herself a cup of coffee. Krystal just made a "mmm" noise as she took a sip of her apple juice. Krystal had never been a coffee person.

"I invited him to the party" Allie added and heard Krystal cough.

"What?" Krystal said and turned in her seat. Allie smiled weakly, "I invited Tyler and Kevin while Derek was standing right there. I didn't want to be rude even though I'm not happy with him" she said and sat across from Krystal who blew through her lips. "I doubt he'll come anyway, Krystal. Honestly, I think we should both stop holding a grudge against him. That was so many years ago. Let's just try and start fresh. You never know. Maybe he really is sorry and he wants to have a second chance" she said as Krystal's eyes looked up to meet hers. "I'm not saying you have to be with him again, but I don't like having so much tension between everyone. Just be his friend" Allie suggested.

Krystal straightened in her chair and lowered her eyes before raising them again, "I tried to be his friend, Allie. He didn't want that. He wanted me out of his life" Krystal said and got to her feet. "I'm going to take a hot bubble bath."

Allie sighed heavily as she watched her friend head for the bathroom. *You really messed her up didn't you, Derek.*

Krystal felt all her muscles relax as she lowered herself into the warm water. Bubble practically covered her as she rested her head against the back of the tub and looked up at the ceiling. Allie's words ran through her head as she lay there. Before Krystal knew it, the water was getting cold and the bubbles had gone away and turned the water murky.

Sighing, Krystal stood and unplugged the tub, then got out and wrapped a towel around herself. Maybe she would give Derek another chance.

Krystal felt better as she walked into her bedroom and got dressed. She wondered whether Derek would come to the party or not and actually looked forward to it. She was smiling and humming to a song on her radio as she turned on her computer and signed into myspace.com. Her smile widened when she saw that she had some new messages from several of her old high school friends.

That following Saturday night, Krystal and Allie's apartment was packed with all their good friends. Food was set out and furniture had been moved to create room to dance.

Krystal smiled as she watched Allie fidget. Tyler and Kevin hadn't arrived yet and Krystal still didn't know if Derek was coming. Earlier that day, she had planned everything she would say to him and hoped that by the end of the night, the tension between them would finally lift as well as the weight on Krystal's shoulders. She also planned on saying a proper goodbye to Derek before he left.

Her heart started to hammer when Tyler and Kevin walked through the door and her hands started to shake as she waited to see Derek walk through the door. When he didn't, her heart continued to hammer - this time in fear - as she walked towards Kevin. Allie had already snagged Tyler.

Kevin turned and smiled when Krystal called his name. "Hey, Krys. What's up?" he asked. "Is Derek coming?" Krystal asked and felt her heart drop when the smile vanished from Kevin's face. "No, sorry. He left this morning. Didn't Allie tell you?" he asked. Krystal's heart stopped as she shook her head. Before Kevin could see the tears, Krystal turned and hurried towards her bedroom. Something seemed to crack inside her, then the tears came. Inside her room, Krystal shut the door and pressed her back to it, then slid to the floor, wrapped her arms around her knees, and sobbed.

Chapter 9

October 2014

"It's still so hard for me to believe that my baby is all grown up and married" Becky told Krystal and flicked at a tear that had slid down her cheek. Twenty-five year old, Krystal smiled as she looked over at her brother and his new wife. Both Becky and Krystal had been delighted when Brian announced he and Amanda were getting married just last year. Now the two of them were newlyweds and trying to find a decent house or apartment to move in to.

The two of them had had it all planned out. Amanda would stay in school and get her master's degree in medicine while Brian worked to help pay for it.

"Come on mom, you're acting like I'm going to get up and leave. Amanda and I are staying right here in Aspen" Brian said and rolled his eyes, but he was smiling.

"I know. It's just hard not having you two in the house anymore. I'm going crazy with it just being me and your father" she said with a smile. Krystal shook her head and smiled back.

When Brian and Amanda left an hour later, Krystal stood to help her mom clean up before she headed back to her own apartment.

"So, how's the job at Dr. Sheperd's?" Becky asked as she handed Krystal a dish to dry. Krystal took it and began drying it with a towel as she smiled. Only Becky could see the twinkle in her daughter's eyes and the slight blush to her cheeks.

"It's going really well. Matt….I mean, Dr. Sheperd has been having me assist him in every surgery he's been doing. I think the other assistants are getting jealous" Krystal said and turned her face away so her mom couldn't read her feelings towards her boss.

Becky didn't have to look at her daughter to see how she felt about Matthew Sheperd. She could hear it in her voice.

When Becky had met the young vet for the first time, her heart had fluttered and she had almost melted from his smile.

He was only twenty-nine which was rare in Aspen. All their vets and doctors looked like they had been around since the town was first discovered.

Matt Sheperd had moved to Aspen to take over for Dr. Wilson who had finally decided to retire at sixty-six due to health problems. From what Krystal had told Becky, all the young, female, veterinary assistances and technicians were in love with the new, tall, and handsome vet. She didn't blame them one bit.

"That's good. Just be careful, honey" Becky said. Krystal couldn't help but laugh. There was nothing she could hide from her mom. "I will, mom. Besides, as soon as I'm ready, I'm starting my own clinic" Krystal replied as she put the dish in the cupboard. Becky just nodded.

The two washed and dried in silence for a while before Krystal broke the silence. "Have Brian and Amanda found a house yet?"

Becky shrugged, "they've been circling and looking. They have a huge pile of flyers on different houses" she replied and chuckled, "I love having your brother over, but he's starting to get as bad as your father, if you know what I mean. Always wanting me to fix him something to eat. The man's twenty-two, but he's acting like he's six again. I do love him though" Becky said and Krystal laughed.

The next morning, Krystal was up early and at the vet clinic a half an hour before her shift started.

The night shifts were just leaving with large cups of coffee in their hands and looking like they were ready to crash.

Aspen Valley Animal Hospital was the only veterinarian office around. Normally it was closed at night, but was always open to emergency cases.

Dr. Sheperd lived in the apartment just above the clinic, and it had several rooms in the back for the people on the night shifts to catch a nap in between cases. It helped all kinds of household pets from rodent to equine and occasionally had an injured wild animal.

With it still being early, the clinic was silent and smelled of cleaner, medicine, and animals. Krystal headed towards the back rooms to store away her purse. She already wore her colorful scrubs with little cartoon dogs and cats.

On her way to the room, Dr. Sheperd came walking down the stairs that led up to his apartment and Krystal felt her heart do a flip in her chest as she stopped to watch him.

He was tall and slim, but muscular, with slightly long black hair that he combed back and green eyes with golden flecks around his pupils. He wore a plain gray t-shirt and jeans and was slipping on his white vet's coat when he looked up and spotted Krystal. He smiled.

"Hey, you're here early" he said as he stepped down from the final step and walked towards her. Krystal's heart was hammering against her ribs as she smiled. "Yeah, I wanted to say goodbye to Gringo before his owners come and take him away from me. It sure feels good to know he's well and healthy enough to go home" Krystal replied and felt her knees turn to jelly when Matt smiled at her warmly. "Well, I'm going to put my purse away, then I'll go see him before we open" she said and hurried away. She could feel Matt's eyes on her as she quickly walked down the hall.

The room was filled with cages of all sizes and

as the animals started to wake, it grew noisy from their hunger whimpers and meows. Krystal walked towards a cage she had visited everyday and smiled when the big tan Great Dane barked excitedly and pawed at the bars of his cage.

"Hey Gringo. Did you miss me? I missed you" Krystal said and knelt down to reach in and rub the dog behind the ears.

Gringo had been on the verge of dying when he had been rushed into the clinic just two weeks before. He had been really sick with a rare canine disease and had had to be kept in a room all by himself so he didn't pass it on to other dogs.

Krystal had been one of the vets who had sat with him and offered comforting words. Once, she had even sat up with him all night just praying he'd make it through.

When the medicine had finally started to kill off the disease, the whole clinic had breathed a sigh of relief. Everyone had fallen in love with the huge Dane and would've been extremely devastated if he hadn't made it. Now, Gringo was healed completely and would be going home in just a few hours.

Gringo licked Krystal's arm, then nudged it with his cold, wet nose which made Krystal laugh and pull it away. "Okay, okay" she said and pulled a dog biscuit from her pocket.

Gringo ate it in one bite and nudged Krystal. "No, that's all you get. You'll be fed soon. See you later, big guy" she said and stood. Just then, one of the veterinary technicians walked in and started to

Only You

fill food and waters so all eyes, including Gringo's, turned to her.

Krystal slipped out of the room and walked out into the waiting area just as the first patient of the day came through the door.

Chapter 10

Aspen was so different, yet so familiar. Several new buildings and homes had been built since he had been there last.

Derek couldn't help but sigh in relief as he drove smoothly down Main Street. First, he was going to look at the property where his new house would be built, then he was going to go by the small apartment he had rented to meet the movers and get moved in.

His parents had been slightly disappointed when he told them he was moving back to Aspen Valley, but they were excited when he told them he was going to build a house and a guest house for whenever they decided to come visit.

As he drove, the people walking on the sidewalks turned and squinted at the small black car and a few pointed and talked to the people beside them. He could already hear what they were saying.

Derek Andrews was back in Aspen Valley.

Krystal smiled when she stepped into the waiting room holding Gringo's leash and watched as his owners and their eight year old son jumped to their feet and hurried over to throw their arms around him.

Krystal slowly handed the leash to the father and returned his smile. The mother looked up and smiled at her too. "Thank you so much for what you've done with Gringo, Krystal. I'm so happy you were the one to take care of him. Tell your mom I say 'hi'" she said.

"Your welcome, Mrs. Nichols and I will" Krystal replied and took the folder that was handed to her.

"Tiki Wyatt" she called and smiled when an elderly lady stood holding a miniature, white poodle. She led Mrs. Wyatt to one of the examining rooms, then proceeded in taking weighing Tiki and taking her temperature.

"I'd just like her to get her yearly check-up and any shots that she needs" Mrs. Wyatt said in a shaky high voice. Krystal looked up and smiled at the elderly lady. She had known Mrs. Wyatt since she was five. Mrs. Wyatt had once run a daycare and Krystal had been one of her regulars back when Becky worked.

"Okay, Mrs. Wyatt. Everything else looks great" Krystal said, then opened a drawer to take out the shots that Tiki needed. Tiki took her shots like a pro, then she and Mrs. Wyatt were able to leave.

Krystal jotted down some notes in Tiki's file before she gave it back to the technicians at the desk.

When she walked back into the back room, Dr. Sheperd waved her over as he was pulling on some latex gloves. "I want you to perform this surgery. I'll be standing next to you the entire time in case you need help" he said.

Krystal's eyes widened in shock which made Dr. Sheperd laugh. "Go on, get ready" he said.

Krystal was still in shock as she got ready to perform surgery on a cat that had been brought in with a broken leg. She had dissected animals before back in high school and college, but she hadn't performed any surgeries yet,

Dr. Sheperd stood by her the entire time. Once she got started, she realized how simple it actually was to her and she ended up not needing as much advice as she thought she would.

As soon as the cat's leg was stitched up and put in a cast, Krystal stripped off her bloodied gloves, surgery scrubs, face mask, and scrub hat, then re-washed her hands and arms before moving onto the next patient.

"Nice job today, Dr. Jacobson" Dr. Sheperd said and laid a hand on her shoulder. His touch sent a shock of electricity running down Krystal's spine, arms, and legs as she turned to face him. *Dr. Jacobson*. It sounded so perfect.

"Thank you, Dr. Sheperd. For everything" she replied. He just smiled and nodded before walking away.

With a bounce in her step, Dr. Jacobson walked down the hall to the waiting room to call in her next patient.

Derek slammed on his brakes and tensed for the impact as he watched the dark streak disappear from his view in front of his car. He felt a thud and heard a yelp, swore under his breath and tore off his seatbelt.

He had been casually driving along when the big black dog had run out in front of him. He had thought it was a bear at first because the dog was so huge.

Throwing open his car door, he quickly got out of the car and rounded to the front praying the stray would get up and run away from the road. He prayed he didn't find a dead dog and felt his breath escape in a sigh of relief when he saw that the dog was still breathing.

It lay in front of his car with it's eyes closed and it's sides heaving. He needed to get this poor animal to a vet and fast.

The dog seemed to weigh a ton when Derek picked it up and carried it around to the passenger side of his car. He laid it down in the back seat, then quickly got back in on the driver's side and turned around to head back into town. Every once in a while he looked in his rearview mirror to see how the dog was doing and swore under his breath again. He felt terrible. This dog might have a family with little kids just waiting for it to come home and play with them and Derek had practically killed it.

Praying there weren't any cop cars around, Derek sped into town and headed towards Aspen Valley Animal Hospital

Krystal was sitting down in the back room eating her lunch and reading a veterinary magazine when one of the vet technicians poked her head in. "Um, Dr. Jacobson, there's a case here that needs emergency care. She isn't one of our patients" she said.

Krystal was instantly to her feet and abandoned her soda and sandwich as she followed the tech to the waiting room.

When she walked into the examining room where the dog had been taken, she stopped dead in her tracks.

The guy sitting on the chair was bent over and had his head in his hands. Krystal didn't need to see his face to know who he was, but she wasn't about to worry about him when an animal who needed her was laying unconscious on the table.

"I already weighed her and took her temperature" the tech said and handed Krystal a paper with the notes, "thank you, Emily, I'll take it from here" Krystal said and walked over to the dog. Still Derek didn't look up.

"Mr. Andrews, I'm Dr. Jacobson. What happened exactly?" Krystal asked as she began examining the dog. She would need to take x-rays to make sure there weren't any broken bones or internal bleeding. The dog was breathing really fast and that concerned her.

Derek was silent for a long time, then his head snapped up as her name sunk in. He stared at her for a long time, but she didn't look at him. Finally after a long moment of silence, she turned to him and he was surprised to see the fury flashing dangerously in her eyes.

"Mr. Andrews. What happened? I need to know" she said. She saw him wince at her tone of voice and how she had addressed him, but he just kept gaping at her.

"Never mind, just go wait in the waiting room and I'll take your dog in for x-rays. What's her name?" Krystal asked and picked the dog off the table.

Derek was surprised at her strength. The dog had seemed too heavy even for him. Finally he muttered, "he's not my dog. He was a stray and ran out in front of me. I don't know if he has any family" he replied. Krystal smirked.

"You can leave if you want and this is a girl dog, not a boy" she said shortly and walked from the room before he could say anymore.

Derek sat in the examining room just staring at the door Krystal and the dog had gone through. Her words and tone of voice ran through his mind and he could feel familiar emotions beginning to resurface at the memory of seeing her standing there just a few feet away in a white vet's lab coat, colorful scrubs, white tennis shoes, and her blonde hair pulled back in a ponytail.

He had also caught a whiff of her perfume which was mixed with the smell of sick animals and medicine.

Shaking his head, he stood and went back out

into the waiting room

Derek vanished from Krystal's mind as she took x-rays of the dog, then turned on the oxygen so she could breathe easier.

As soon as the x-rays were developed, she stuck them up and examined them, then sighed heavily. There were no broken bones or internal bleeding.

Krystal walked over to where the dog lay and laid a hand on her fluffy black coat. She was a Tibetan Mastiff and a gorgeous one for that matter.

She didn't wear a collar so Krystal decided to send out a FOUND flyer and see if anyone had lost her. For the mean time, Krystal would keep her under close watch.

Krystal smiled when the dog's large brown eyes flickered up and looked up at her. Kneeling down, Krystal scratched her head.

"Hey sweetie. You're safe now" she murmured in a soothing tone and smiled when the dog's tongue flicked out and touched her hand.

After giving the dog one final pat, Krystal walked back out to the main desk and ignored the eyes she felt on her.

"Emily, make up a folder for the Mastiff that was just brought in and make up some found flyers. Also, call the pound and see if there were any calls about a four year old, female, Tibetan Mastiff" Krystal said and the tech nodded and went to work.

Just then, Dr. Sheperd walked out and laid a hand on Krystal's shoulder.

"I saw the dog that was just brought in. She's

Only You

looking much better" he said and Krystal smiled up at him, "yeah, I'm going to put her in a cage in a minute and see if she's hungry" she replied. Dr. Sheperd nodded and called in his next patient.

Krystal sent a glance over the waiting room and was surprised to see Derek still sitting there. Not wanting to leave him out, she crossed the room and stuffed her hands in her vet's coat.

He looked up with an expression that took her by surprise.

His eyes were bright with tears as he looked up and when he whispered, "I'm sorry" she wasn't sure if he meant he was sorry about the dog or what had happened between them.

She sat in the chair beside him.

"The dog is doing really well. She's just in shock but we have her on oxygen to help her breathing. There are no broken bones or internal injuries. We're going to try and find her family and if she isn't a missing pet, I'll have her given to a good home. Unless you would like to adopt her?" Krystal said and Derek's head snapped up.

He stared at her, then shook his head.

"Okay, Mr. Andrews. You may leave now. I'm sure you're very busy" Krystal said and stood. She could tell it hurt and confused him that she called him Mr. Andrews and not Derek, but she honestly didn't care at the moment. She had patients to see. Patients that depended on her. Patients that didn't run from their problems and pleaded for her to help them.

When she walked back out into the waiting

room later that afternoon to call in her next patient, Derek was gone.

"I don't want to leave her" Krystal said as she sat beside the dog and scratched her ears. She was off the oxygen now and was thumping her tail and rolling over so Krystal could rub her belly.

Matt knelt down in front of Krystal and gave the dog's head a pat.

"Then take her home with you. I've done it with several of my patients. You're apartment is zoned for a dog. Let her stay with you until her family is found" he suggested.

Krystal smiled as she thought about that and nodded, "I think I will."

Chapter 11

When Krystal opened the door to her apartment later that afternoon carrying bags from Petco, the dog walked right in and walked around sniffing everything.

"I sure hope you're housetrained. I don't need a dog going on the carpet and getting me in trouble by the manager" Krystal said closing the door with her foot.

The dog turned and looked up at her with her head tilted to the side as Krystal walked into her small kitchen and set the bags on the counter. She then opened the slider so the dog could go out into the tiny back yard to explore.

Krystal stood and watched the dog for a while before turning and pulling out the new food and water bowl she bought and filled them up. She had also gotten Science Diet dog food, since Dr. Sheperd had recommended it, some chew toys and bones, and a large dog bed.

Krystal smiled when the dog scratched at the window. She walked over to open the door. Looking out at the dirt, Krystal was relieved to see that the dog had already done her business. She closed the slider and turned to see the dog jumping up on her couch.

"No. No. Get down" Krystal said without raising her voice too much. She pointed towards the dog bed she had laid in the corner and couldn't help but smile when the dog looked up at her with sad eyes.

"Now, don't give me that look. No dogs on the furniture" Krystal said and clapped her hands. With a small grunt, the dog hopped off the couch and walked over to the bed where she circled three times before laying down and resting her head between her paws and looking up at Krystal.

"Don't worry, I'll find your family" she told the dog and turned. "I hope" she added in a whisper. She also didn't know how long her landlord would allow her to keep the dog at her place.

When she had moved in, she had become friends with the owners of the apartment complex. They had given in and told her she could keep the dog for however long it took to find her owners, but she knew the dog couldn't stay permanently and Krystal didn't have the money to pay for a house just yet.

Most of the people who lived in the nearby apartments had cats or toy dog breeds. The yards were far too small for a dog of this size and Krystal worried she'd feel cramped.

"I might have to find somewhere else for you to stay. You'll stay with me for a couple nights, though. It'll be nice to have the company" she said and turned to start making dinner.

Krystal took the dog with her to work the next morning hoping to find the owners waiting there for her. They weren't. In fact, no one had reported a missing dog. Now it would be up to Krystal to find a good adoptive home.

"I can't keep her at the apartment. My landlord is giving me a few days to be nice, but I can't keep her even though I want to" Krystal told Dr. Sheperd before patients began arriving.

Dr. Sheperd looked over to where the dog sat in one of the cages looking out at them with a hopeful expression.

"Why don't you give her to that guy who brought her in. I heard he's building a good sized house on a few acres of land. A guy like him could use a dog" he suggested and Krystal's eyes widened.

"That's not a bad idea. Thanks, Dr. Sheperd. I'll call him today" she replied feeling a little nervous towards the thought of calling Derek.

"Your welcome. And Krystal, call me Matt before and after business hours" he said with a smile.

Krystal felt her heart leap as she smiled weakly back, "okay…Matt" she replied and he grinned.

Once Matt walked away, Krystal picked up the phone and was about to dial when she realized she didn't have Derek's number.

She flipped through the folder that had been made on the dog and sighed in relief when she saw one of the technicians had scribbled down Derek's cell.

With shaky hands, Krystal dialed the number and brought it to her ear after taking a deep breath and trying to steady her pounding heart. This would be the first time she had called Derek in years.

Derek frowned when he read the unfamiliar number on his cell. He flipped it open and brought it to his ear wondering who would be calling him this early in the morning.

"Hello."

"Hi, Mr. Andrews. This is Dr. Jacobson over at the animal hospital. No one has claimed the dog you brought in and we were wondering if you would like to adopt her before we try to find another home?"

Derek froze as that all too familiar voice filled his ear and warmed his heart.

"Um, hello, Krys….I mean, Dr. Jacobson. I don't…" he was at a loss for words. Krystal had caught him off guard and she sounded so normal that he didn't know what to say.

"Please, call me Derek?" he heard himself ask.

There was a long pause, "yes….Derek" Krystal said.

Derek rubbed his thumb against his temple and closed his eyes. What should he do? He really didn't want a dog right now, but taking this one might let him see Krystal more. *But you haven't even thought of having a dog*, he told himself.

"I'm sorry. I'm currently staying in an apartment complex that doesn't allow dogs. I would feel better if you found her a better home" he said.

Was that really him talking? He didn't feel like he had control over his voice or his words.

Krystal hesitated.

"Alright. Thank you for your time. Goodbye, Mr. Andrews" she said.

"Krystal, wait" he called into the phone, but he was too late. She had already hung up.

Krystal sighed when she put the phone down, then turned to the computer to find someone who would add the dog to their adoption program. She definitely didn't want to send her to the pound. They ended up putting animals down when they weren't adopted fast enough.

She still hadn't found anyone when the technicians and patients began walking in. With a sigh, she got off the computer and took the first patient into the examining room. Maybe she'd put up some flyers and see if anyone wanted the dog. With another heavy sigh, Krystal pushed the dog from her mind and went to work.

As the day came to an end, Krystal sighed in relief and grabbed a bottle of water. Her last patient had just left and now she was hoping to sit and relax for a while. Resting her head back, Krystal closed her eyes.

"You know the boss wouldn't be very happy if he walked in and saw you sleeping on the job" a deep, teasing voice said. Krystal smiled and opened her eyes to look up at Matt, who stood over her looking down at her. "Then don't tell him" she replied and he grinned.

She was surprised when Matt plopped down next to her. "You got any hot dates tonight?" he asked after a long pause.

It took Krystal by surprise and she almost shot water out of her nose when she went to take a drink. Matt just smiled.

"U-um, no."

"Would you like to have dinner with me?" Matt asked casually.

Now Krystal turned and raised her eyebrows, "I thought dating your boss wasn't allowed" she said. This time he raised his eyebrows.

"Who says this is a personal date? What if it's a business date?" he asked in a serious tone. Krystal smiled and looked away, "I might be able to do that" she said. Just then her eyes landed on the dog.

"What should I do with her?" Krystal asked motioning towards the cage.

Matt looked over and smiled, "she can probably be moved to the back kennels until we find her a good home. Mike takes excellent care of the dogs and cats back there" Matt replied and Krystal nodded in agreement.

As soon as the dog was settled in one of the kennels, Krystal and Matt walked out to her car. He held the door open for her as she climbed in.

"I'll be by to get you at seven-thirty. That way you have an hour and a half to get ready. Oh, and dress casual" he said and closed the door for her. She waved, then drove off.

All the way home, her heart hammered against her ribs in anticipation. What would it be like to date Dr. Matthew Sheperds? Was it really a date or just business? She was sure it was a date.

When she got home, she rushed upstairs to take a shower and wondered if an hour and a half would really be enough time.

Matt showed up at exactly seven-twenty nine and knocked.

Krystal had just finished getting ready and examined herself in the mirror one last time before heading down to let him in.

They both took each other by surprise.

Matt had shaved and combed his hair back. Krystal could smell his aftershave and it made her legs weaken. It smelled so good. So....masculine. He wore a close fitting gray t-shirt and baggy jeans with his usual tennis shoes and held flowers in his hand.

Krystal had been surprised to see the flowers, but when he handed them to her and watched her sniff them, she felt herself falling in love with him.

He was feeling the same as he followed her into her apartment and watched her search for something to put the flowers in.

"I haven't had flowers in so long. I swear I had a vase somewhere…"

He could hear her voice, but not the words. All he heard was the sweet tone of it as he looked her up and down.

She wore a close-fitting navy blue t-shirt and tight blue jeans. Her blonde hair fell down her back in spiral curls and stopped just between her shoulder blades.

He had never seen her outside the vet's clinic so he had never seen her in regular clothes and usually her hair was pulled up in a ponytail to keep it out of her face. Now, it hung down and framed her face and he realized just how beautiful Krystal Jacobson really was.

Matt had sworn to himself he wouldn't get emotionally attached to any of the people he worked with, but it had been hard to stick with that rule when Krystal walked into the clinic asking for a job. Matt still wondered whether or not it had been love at first sight.

Krystal turned to see Matt staring at her with a warm expression on his face that made her knees weaken even more. She held the vase and flowers in her hands and hoped they didn't get too shaky or else she'd drop the vase her mother had given to her.

"Thank you for the flowers. They're lovely" she said in a somewhat shaky voice.

Only You

Matt snapped back to reality and replaced the warm look with a friendly smile.

"I'm glad you like them. I didn't know what to get" he replied hoping he sounded casual. She smiled, "I like anything I'm given."

After Krystal set the flowers on the kitchen table, Matt took her hand and led her out of the apartment and over to his car. Unlike the doctor in Aspen Valley, who drove a BMW, Matt owned a big Ford truck. It was a newer model, but it was clear to Krystal that he tried hard not to show off his money. She liked that a lot.

Matt took her up to Sacramento, which was only about forty-five minutes to an hour from Aspen Valley, and pulled into the Outback Steakhouse parking lot.

Krystal now understood why he had said casual.

Growing up, she had heard of Outback, but she had never been there because her parents hadn't wanted to drive that far just to go to dinner so she was excited as Matt helped her from the truck, then led her up to the front, double doors.

It was packed inside and the smell of cooking food filled the air. Soft rock music played in the background and in the bar area, a large flat screen TV was mounted up on the wall and was turned to a baseball game.

"Have you been here before?" Krystal asked after Matt put his name in. The hostess had smiled at him as if she knew him. Matt smiled and nodded, "I come here almost every weekend to have dinner. Usually I'm with a few of my friends who live here in Sacramento" he replied and took her hand again when his name was called.

The food was delicious and conversation with Matt was easy. At first they talked about the animals they had seen that day and slowly Krystal began seeing Matt as Matt and not as the head vet and boss of the clinic.

"I heard you've lived in Aspen all your life" Matt said as he picked up a chili covered cheese fry and popped it in his mouth. Krystal picked one up herself as she nodded.

"I lived in Davis for a while, but something happened and I came back down here to go to college" she replied and looked up to see Matt frown in interest.

"What happened?"

"Normally I wouldn't say, but I feel like I can tell you. I had a boyfriend who was going to UC Davis with me. He was studying to be a doctor. Anyway, when we came home to visit, he cheated on me with an old classmate. When I found out, he blamed it all on me because I wouldn't go to bed with him. My parents kicked him out and I moved back here to attend AVU" Krystal said and shrugged her shoulders. She was completely over Jason and felt nothing, even when Matt gave her a look of sympathy.

"I'm sorry. That must've been horrible for you" he said and she shrugged again. "It was when it happened, but I've forgotten all about him" she replied.

"What about you?" she asked. She was dying to know some personal things about him.

"Let's see. I lived in Seattle, Washington before I moved here. I lived there for most of my life. I have a step mom and a dad who are both enjoying retirement down in Arizona. My biological mom lives in Florida and I talk to her occasionally. She ran out on my dad when I was only seven. My dad hasn't been able to forgive her since she ran off with his ex-best friend. I have a younger half sister, Kaylee, who will be turning nineteen in a few months. Hmm, I got my Associate's degree at Cal Poly Pomona, then both my Bachelor and Master degrees at UC Davis. After college, I moved back up to Washington until I learned Dr. Wilson was retiring. I remember visiting Aspen Valley while I was attending UC Davis and thought about moving down there" Matt said.

All Krystal could do was smile, he had told her much more than she had expected he would.

"What about you?" Matt asked leaning across and smiling warmly at her. "I already know about your tragic ex-boyfriend, but I don't know anything else."

Krystal smiled back, then took a deep breath. He had told her a lot and she felt it was only fair to do the same. Besides, she liked to get the truth out when she could. Something she had learned after her relationship with Derek.

"Let's see. I was born in Aspen and lived there all the way until I was eighteen, then I went up to Davis for that short time before I came back. I've been here ever since. My mom is from England so she has a little bit of a British accent. She met my dad when she came to the United States to attend school as a foreign exchange student in her senior year. They fell in love, then she came back for college and became a citizen. My parents' names are Rebecca and Jeff Jacobson. I have a younger brother, Brian, who just got married" Krystal replied and shrugged her shoulders.

"Any other ex-boyfriends or husbands?" Matt asked and grinned when Krystal's eyes widened in horror. She laughed when he realized he was joking about the husband part.

"I had a few short relationships throughout middle and high school. Those only lasted a few weeks to a month."

Here Krystal hesitated and wondered if she should tell Matt about Derek. He gave her an encouraging look to continue.

"There was one boy who lasted longer than a month. We were together for a year and a half and were deeply in love. At least, I was deeply in love. We were just two love struck teenagers already making plans to get married and start a life together after high school and college" she said and dropped her eyes, then raised them.

"What happened?" Matt asked and Krystal suddenly realized his hand was covering hers on the table. She looked up into his eyes and shrugged.

"He got to be too stressed out. His dad left so he became responsible for the family and his dad's business as well as keeping up his grades so he could graduate. He told me in a letter that he needed time away and I understood that and accepted it even though I didn't want to let him go. What hurt was how he treated me afterward. I disappeared from his life completely as if I had never existed and when I tried to talk to him, he pushed me away and told me to get on with my life because he was getting on with his. So I did. It was so painful at first and I cried for two straight weeks, then on and off over the following months. I started dating different guys just to help get him off my mind, but none of those guys lasted more than a week because I was seeing Derek's face instead of theirs."

Krystal stopped and closed her eyes for just a moment before opening them and offering Matt a smile.

"Do you still love him?" Matt asked in interest.

The question took Krystal by surprise, but she quickly shook her head, "that was then. I've gotten over him" she replied, then added, "what about you?"

Matt seemed to hesitate as well.

"There was this girl..." he began and hesitated again.

"Well, I'm glad it was a girl or else I'd be wondering what I'm doing here" she said and Matt laughed. Krystal saw him relax and as he began, she could tell it was easier for him.

"We were high school sweethearts like you and, what was his name? Derek. Anyway, we stayed together even though she was attending school up in Washington and I was down in Pomona. We would call each other every night or e-mail. When I was visiting, we'd go out to dinner and spend as much time with each other as we could. We were also planning our future wedding and one year when I was visiting for Christmas, I proposed to her. It would still be several years before either of us could get married because of school, but our parents approved and when I asked her, she started crying and leaped into my arms."

Here, Matt hesitated and Krystal could tell what was coming wasn't good by the look on his face.

"About a month later, we both grew to be really busy and soon our phone calls and e-mails were dropping to every other day, to two times a week, to once a week. Finally, they stopped for a while and I looked forward to going home and seeing her. I made a surprise visit and walked in on her in bed with another guy in her dorm room. She tried to explain, but I wouldn't let her. I was too hurt and shocked. Finally, she started yelling, then threw her ring at me. That was the last time I saw her. I finished college and moved here. I think moving here was an escape along with getting a new job" Matt said.

Krystal was silent for a moment, then she rested her other hand over the one that covered his in a

Only You

sympathetic gesture. The two of them stared into each others eyes without saying anything. Krystal swore she felt something tug deep inside her, but the feeling disappeared when the waiter arrived and their gazes turned away from each other.

As they ate their main meal, Krystal couldn't help but think how the two of them had suffered almost the same way. Matt's story was definitely more heartbreaking than hers and she felt her heart go out to him. How could anybody do something like that to a sweet and handsome guy like him? Then again, how could someone do something so mean to a kind, caring girl like her? Neither of them had done anything to receive that kind of punishment.

After dinner, Krystal and Matt went for a walk along the shops that lined the streets. He had taken her hand as soon as they had left the restaurant and had laced his fingers with hers. This time though, the touch seemed deeper than when they had walked in.

When Matt walked Krystal to her front door later that evening, Krystal couldn't help but feel butterflies fluttering in her stomach. Would he kiss her goodnight? The thought made her nervous, yet hopeful.

She stopped at her door and fished in her purse for her keys. Her hands were shaking so bad that she almost dropped them when she finally pulled them out. With a smile, she looked up at Matt and felt her heart leap. He was looking down at her with almost as much nerves shooting through his body and he had to stuff his hands in his pockets. He wanted to kiss her, but he didn't want to rush anything.

"Well, goodnight, Krystal" he said and took a step back. Some disappointment flashed in her eyes, but it vanished when she smiled. "Goodnight, Matt. Thank you so much for tonight" she said. *What the heck*, she thought as she stood on her tip toes and kissed his cheek. Both felt their cheeks flush as Krystal turned to unlock her door. "I-I guess I'll see you tomorrow" Matt said, his eyes still wide in surprise as the spot on his cheek where she had kissed him grew warm and tingly. "Yep. See you" Krystal replied and sent him a warm smile over her shoulder before she stepped inside and turned. They smiled at each other, then Krystal slowly closed the door.

While she leaned against the back of the door, staring off into space with a dreamy smile on her face, Matt walked calmly towards his car even though he felt like leaping in the air. He didn't know what it was about Krystal that made him want to do something like that. He hadn't been so excited about a kiss since his first kiss when he was sixteen.

With a smile still plastered to her face, Krystal floated up the stairs to get ready for bed even though she knew it would be hard for her to fall asleep.

Chapter 12

The next morning, everything went back to being business even though Krystal caught Matt smiling at her several times when no one was looking. She just blushed, smiled back, then hurried off to tend to one of her patients.

One of her good friends, Amy noticed what was going on between the two though and she smiled. Later, when Krystal wasn't busy, Amy pulled her aside.

"Details. What's going on between you and Dr. Sheperd?" Amy asked with a grin. Krystal smiled guiltily back, "what?" she asked and Amy laughed. "Come on, Krystal. I've known you since kindergarten. I know something's going on" Amy said.

The two had known each other since kindergarten, but they hadn't always been friends. Amy hadn't been nice to Krystal that much when they were younger and it hadn't been until high school that Amy finally started talking to Krystal like a friend, even though she had been a cheerleader.

"Let's just say we had a date last night that was strictly business" Krystal replied quietly. Amy raised her eyebrows, "yeah right." Krystal laughed, "okay, okay. We went on a date last night and it went really well" Krystal replied as she looked through one of her patient's file. Amy beamed, "it's nice to hear that you're finally getting back into dating." Krystal just shrugged with a smile, "let's see how long it lasts" she replied before heading to the waiting room to call in her next patient.

As Derek drove through town, he thought strongly about stopping by the animal hospital to see Krystal. He needed to fix things between them even if it was too late. He knew he'd feel better once he told Krystal what was on his mind, but he couldn't find the courage to pull into the parking lot and go inside.

Cursing under his breath when someone honked at him, Derek continued down the road. An idea suddenly flashed in his brain and made him slam on his brakes. The guy behind him called Derek a fowl name as Derek made a quick U turn and headed back towards the clinic.

Krystal was surprised to see Derek since he had no real reason to be there. She was weighing a very unhappy dog when he walked in and got distracted. Sensing her distraction, the dog made a dash towards the door, but was stopped when Krystal grabbed his collar and coaxed him back.

Derek said something to the technician behind the desk and out of the corner of her eye, Krystal saw Emily nod and motion towards Krystal. Derek turned and waited until she was finished with the dog before stepping forward.

"If you still have that dog, I'd be happy to look at her" he said and smiled gently. Krystal straightened as she handed the folder over the counter to Emily and shoved her hands in the pocket's of her white lab coat.

Derek's eyes took her in. She wore a tight, gray t-shirt, jeans, and sneakers. Her hair was pulled up in a ponytail and showed off her graceful neck, elegant shoulders, and collarbone. Derek had always thought she was the most gorgeous woman he had ever seen and he was sorry for giving her up and making things so hard for her over the past several years.

Krystal's eyes, eyes that still made his blood boil, looked around the waiting room, then turned back to him. "I can take you back real quick, but I have patients, Mr. Andrews" she replied and turned to lead him towards the back.

"Please, Krystal, call me Derek" he said quietly. He knew she had heard him, but she didn't say anything as she led him through another door and into the back kennels where a few dogs were housed.

They barked excitedly at their visitors. "This is where we keep the dogs who are brought in from the street. They're all entered into the adoption program. We don't euthanize any animals here like they do at the pound" she said making sure her voice sounded businesslike.

She stopped at the cage where the dog he had

brought in was sitting patiently near the gate.

Derek knelt in front of her and pressed his hand flat against the chain link fence. The dog sniffed his hand through the fence and gave it a small lick before turning her eyes to Krystal.

Krystal couldn't help but watch Derek. Something was on his mind and it had nothing to do with the dog.

"Were you wanting to adopt her?" Krystal asked, "or any of the others?" she added.

Derek stood and turned to look at her. Old feelings were stirring deep inside him again, "I actually wanted to come talk to you, Krystal, but I didn't have a good enough excuse to just drop in while you were working" he said quietly.

Her heart leaped. So many years ago, she had been praying for this moment, but now she just couldn't handle it.

"I'm sorry, Derek. I'm working and very busy. I can't talk right now. Besides, there's nothing to talk about. We both moved on, just like you wanted" she said and he heard a pang of hurt in her voice as she opened the door for him. He wanted to persuade her to talk to him so he could tell her what he was feeling, but it was clear he was being dismissed and he really didn't want to pull her away from her work. Nodding slowly, he walked by and followed as she led him back to the waiting area. "Goodbye, Mr. Andrews" she said kindly.

Just then, a woman came rushing in carrying a puppy and looking frantic. Derek jumped out of the way, then watched as Krystal instantly sprang into action and forgot about him.

Derek walked from the clinic and towards his car. A part of him wanted to just forget about her. She had made it clear she had forced him out of her mind. He didn't blame her. After what he had done to her, he wouldn't want to remember him either. He was still in love with her and couldn't just give her up when he was willing to do whatever it took to get her back. With a heavy sigh, Derek got in his car and drove off.

While Derek was slowly heading home, Krystal was leaning over the puppy performing the biggest surgery she had ever performed while the terrified owner sat out in the waiting room.

Apparently, the puppy had been attacked by a much bigger dog and had multiple injuries. Krystal was going to do everything in her power to save him.

When the heart line suddenly went flat, Krystal's own heart felt like it stopped as her assistants quickly worked to revive the puppy. She stood back and stared at the monitor hoping to see the heart start back up. After several times of trying to bring the puppy around, Krystal pulled down her face mask and stared at the small animal with tears misting in her eyes. She had always known it would hurt when she lost one of her patients for the first time, she just didn't think it would hurt this much.

The assistants stepped back and began clearing

the room as Krystal walked over and laid a hand on the puppy. "I'm sorry" she whispered, then turned to go inform the owner.

One of the assistants took Mrs. Danbury back so she could say goodbye to her puppy while Krystal escaped and locked herself in the back room. Tears rolled down her cheeks as she stared at the ceiling. All she could see was Mrs. Danbury's eyes when Krystal delivered the news.

A soft knock had Krystal lifting her head to see Matt step in the room. She wiped at her tears as he walked over and knelt in front of her. "It wasn't your fault, Krystal. I don't think there was anything anyone could do. It was too late when the puppy was brought in" he said and gathered Krystal in his arms.

She pressed her face to his chest and finished crying, then pulled away and dried her face, then offered him a teary smile. He smiled back and couldn't help but feel his heart tug as he looked into her shiny, red-rimmed eyes. He was falling in love with her faster than he was ready for.

"Come on, we have more patients waiting out there for us" he said and helped her to her feet.

They embraced for a minute before they headed back to the waiting room. Work at Aspen Valley Animal Hospital continued as usual.

Krystal let out a heavy sigh of relief when she walked through her front door and turned on the lights. She was finally home and looking forward to soaking in a hot bubble bath. The air outside had dropped several degrees since the night before and she was shivering slightly as she hurried inside.

She dropped her purse by her phone whose message light was blinking and stood for a while staring at it while she tried to decide whether to go ahead and listen to her messages or wait until she was finished with her bath in case one of them needed to be called back as soon as possible.

Shrugging, Krystal headed for her upstairs bathroom where she started the bath and poured salts and oils into the steaming water. Next, she walked back into her bedroom and grabbed the tank top and baggy plaid pants she wore to bed, then stripped and slowly sank into the tub.

Within minutes, she was completely relaxed and drowsy. She had really missed doing this.

Almost a half an hour later, Krystal got out, wrapped a towel around her body and her head, began drying, then changed into her tank top and pants and combed her wet hair. Normally, she blow dried it, but since she didn't have to go anywhere, she decided to let it dry on it's own.

She was looking forward to making herself a sandwich, and maybe some hot apple cider, and curling up on the couch with a blanket and watching movies until she fell asleep.

Krystal chose a romance and curled up on the couch. She suddenly wished she had an animal to keep her company. Maybe she'd adopt one of the cat's from the clinic. The thought vanished from her mind as tears suddenly blurred her vision. *The Notebook* had been Krystal's favorite since she was in high school. Back then it had been her favorite because the two young characters had reminded her too much of herself and Derek when they were young and in love. She pushed him from her mind as she felt her eyelids grow heavy. The day had finally caught up with her.

With the following day being Krystal's day off, she stayed at home cleaning and watching TV.

She grew bored by noon and decided to go into town to go shopping. She had needed new clothes for a few months and it was starting to get colder as they entered November.

Krystal parked her car in the small shopping center's parking lot and wrapped her coat tightly around her as she started towards the store that had been her favorite place to shop since she was a teenager.

The small American Eagle Outfitters was the only name brand clothes store in Aspen Valley. Krystal, along with every other teenager or young adult in town, would either shop there or drive all the way up to Sacramento to shop in other name brand stores like Abercrombie and Fitch, Hollister, etc.

When she left the store a half an hour later, she was carrying two bags filled with winter clothes.

The purchases had been expensive, but Krystal had had so much money in her checking account lately that she had needed to use a little bit for clothes.

She sat in her car and waited for the heater to fill the car with warm air as she studied the dark clouds that were gathering quickly. The news had predicted rain and possibly some snow.

Even though she had never enjoyed the cold, Krystal was looking forward to having snow again. Aspen Valley always looked like it should be put on a Christmas card in the winter.

Chapter 13

Excited barks and pleading meows greeted Krystal when she walked into the kennels of Aspen Valley Pound. Dogs pressed their noses and paws to the fence and cats rubbed against the bars of their cages.

It had always been hard for Krystal to come here because she always wanted to adopt every single one of the pets and get them out of danger of being euthanized.

One of the workers at the pound started to follow Krystal, but she waved them off and said she just wanted to look. She was really here to find a new pet, she just didn't like being followed and watched as she studied each of the poor animals.

Krystal entered the room that held the cats and breathed in the scent of cat food and dirty kitty litter. Some cats just watched her while others rubbed their bodies and faces against the bars. Krystal stuck her fingers in the cages of the friendly ones to scratch their chins or necks and smiled when they purred and leaned into her.

"If I could, I'd take all of you" she whispered and moved on. Why couldn't that day be the day when the pound only had a few cats? Why did it have to be packed so Krystal felt guilty about taking only one?

She kept going back to one cage in particular. This cat was underweight and had a ragged looking tabby coat. When he opened his eyes and looked at her, he had one gray eye and one yellow eye. All the other cats had a healthy weight and were friendly to where Krystal was sure they'd be adopted quickly, but this cat worried her and as she stroked his small neck, she felt herself becoming attached.

"You're coming home with me" she whispered. She wanted to get him on a better diet and she wanted to examine him and give him any shots he may need.

Just then, one of the handlers walked in and Krystal turned, "I think I'll take him" she said without smiling.

The handler looked towards the cat and grimaced, "are you sure. He's schedule to be put down later this afternoon" she said turning her eyes back to Krystal whose expression hardened, "then I'd like to get him out of here as quickly as possible and I want a copy of all his shots and examinations" she said with an icy tone. She hadn't meant to ⊦ mean, the pound just seemed to put her in a ' mood.

The woman nodded slowly, "I'll go get ´ pers and a carrier" she said and turned.

Krystal thanked her, then turned back

who was now looking at her with eyes that seemed to be thanking her. She smiled, then opened the cage herself and picked the cat up.

He was much too skinny and didn't fight as she set him on a nearby table to examine him herself.

His eyes were clear and his gums were a healthy color, but it was clear he was suffering from starvation and dehydration.

The handler walked back in and looked surprised to see Krystal holding the cat and stroking its head. His eyes were closed and Krystal could feel him purring quietly.

Once he was in the carrier, Krystal followed the handler back to the main room where she signed the adoption papers and looked over his shot record. Inside she was seething in anger. The poor cat was way behind on his shots.

"You're wasting your time with that one. He was getting close to dying anyway" someone muttered.

Krystal's head snapped up and her eyes flashed dangerously. She remained silent though and that seemed to surprise everyone in the room. Her look had been enough for them.

As soon as she got home, she let the cat out and put down some food and water.

She had gone by the clinic to have Matt look over the cat as well, then he had been given his shots. Other than being skinny and dehydrated, the cat was perfectly healthy and young.

Krystal had grabbed a bag of the cat food Matt suggested, then hurried home before he kicked her out for being at work on her day off.

Now she stood watching the cat slowly eat the new food and frowned when he lost his appetite and walked over to lay down. She was determined to get this cat healthy again.

Derek took a deep breath as he lifted his phone and punched in the number he thought he had forgotten. He just prayed Krystal hadn't gotten a new cell phone.

It rang three times before she picked up and for a minute he debated whether or not to hang up.

"Hello." Her voice sounded irritated as she repeated the greeting.

Krystal was curled up on her couch stroking the cat, whom she had named Elvis, and was about to hang up when the shaky voice said, "Krystal. Hi. It's me, Derek."

Krystal froze, "oh, hi. Um, how'd you get this number?" she asked. "I used to call it all the time" Derek replied. He sounded exactly the same as he had so many years ago.

On the other side, Derek was thinking the same thing, but unlike Krystal, he was pacing around his small kitchen.

"I know you don't want to speak to me, but I

was wondering if we could start over. You know, as friends. Just friends" he said a little too quickly. His heart was hammering and his hands were shaking. This was how he had reacted when he had called her to ask her out.

He clenched his free hand into his fist and shoved it in his pants pocket only to pull it back out when he started making the keys in his pocket jingle.

Krystal was silent. She didn't know what to say. Why hadn't she just ignored the call instead of answering to see who the number belonged to?

"Derek, I tried to make us that, but you didn't want it" she said quietly. She was relieved with the fact that she wasn't feeling anything yet.

"I know. I made a big mistake, Krystal. I want to fix things between us. Can we just start over. As friends?" he asked.

Krystal wanted to tell him off and hang up. She had finally hardened her heart against him and didn't want it being softened again so he could go and break it all over again. But then, she wasn't one to hold grudges and she didn't want to act like a stubborn little kid when she was an adult. She needed to act like an adult.

On the other line, Derek had stopped pacing, but his heart was still hammering as he listened to the silence on the other line. For a minute he wondered if she had hung up on him, but the dial tone never came.

"I'd like that" Krystal said quietly, but without feeling.

Derek's heart almost stopped, then it leaped and filled with joy inside his chest. He wanted to do a little dance, but he'd feel and look retarded.

"Thank you, Krystal. How about we get some lunch on your next day off? We can talk and catch up" he suggested.

"Don't push it, Derek. I'll be your friend, but I'm not ready to put all my trust in you again just yet" she replied quietly.

His heart sank a little at that as he remembered a time when she had trusted him with her life. But he had gone and ruined that for both of them.

Straightening he tightened his grip on the phone. He would fix everything he had done wrong. Maybe he wouldn't have Krystal back the way he hoped, but he'd at least have her as a friend.

"Okay. I'll talk to you later, Krys. Bye" he said. Krystal thought about correcting him since the nickname sent feelings reeling in her body, but instead she just said, "okay, bye", then hung up.

She stared at her phone for a long time replaying the conversation over in her head. She hadn't wanted to feel any past feelings resurface, but they had as soon as Derek had asked if they could be friends.

Krystal would be his friend because she wasn't cruel enough to do to him what he had done to her, but he would know just what he did to her and how hard it was going to be to get her to fully trust him again.

She also didn't want him thinking he could get

her fully back. She had seen the affection in his eyes when he had come to the clinic a few days ago and she just couldn't handle that thought at the moment. Besides, she was with Matt now.

Chapter 14

A month later, Krystal stood in the post office going through her mail and tossing the junk in the trash which sat nearby.

Outside the cold, December wind howled and blew snow flakes everywhere. The streets and yards already had several inches of snow, so cars were driving slower than usual and many of the drivers had put their chains around their tires.

Krystal wore a long-sleeved shirt under her heavy winter coat that had fur around the hood, jeans, thick socks, and light brown Ugg boots.

Her hair hung down around her face from under the beanie she wore and despite the gloves on her hands, her fingers were freezing.

Gathering all her good mail, Krystal took a deep breath then stepped outside just to have that breath be taken away from her as the icy wind slammed into her and made her take a step back.

The snow flakes stung her cheeks as she hurried down the walk towards her car and made it hard for her to see and make sure she didn't slip on any ice.

Normally they had somewhat warm and sunny winter days, but today was one of the cold, stormy days when everyone stayed home with fires in their fireplaces and mugs of hot beverages keeping their hands warm.

Krystal was looking forward to doing just that, but first she had to drive slowly and carefully so she didn't get into an accident.

As she drove home, she wondered if her date with Matt that night would be cancelled. Earlier when she had left, he had been really busy. Normally on days like this one, no one came to the clinic and everyone ended up leaving early. Not Matt. He had had piles of paperwork on his desk and when she had asked him if he wanted her to stick around and help, he had waved her on and told her a little sharply to just go home.

Krystal sighed as she remembered how stiff and short he had been over the past few days. He was wanting to add on to the clinic and was having a hard time with the people who would be doing most of the construction for him and he was afraid they wouldn't have much money once it was finally completed.

Once at home, Krystal set down her purse and her mail and quickly stepped over Elvis before she stepped on the cat, who had rushed over to rub against her ankles.

Over the past month, Elvis had finally gained weight and looked healthier than before. He and Krystal had also formed a strong bond and she didn't know what she'd do if she didn't have him there to greet her when she got home after a long, tiring day.

"Come on, Elvis. I'm going to pull out the decorations. You'll like playing with the ornaments" she said.

Just the other day, Krystal had finally gone to the store and bought herself a small plastic Christmas tree for her apartment, ornaments, a wreath for her front door, lights, and other small Christmas decorations. This would be her first year in her apartment decorating it.

Krystal was stringing the lights around the tree and trying to make sure Elvis wasn't chewing on the wires when her front door opened and Matt walked in. He stood and watched her with a smile as she got herself tangled, then stepped forward and helped her.

"Oh. I didn't know you were here. You scared me. How'd you get in?" she asked looking up and giving him a smile. He smiled back and leaned down to kiss her.

"Your front door was open. I knocked once, but then I heard you singing to your music which is loud enough so you couldn't hear. I tried your door and it was unlocked so I let myself in" he replied and helped her finish wrapping the lights around the tree.

Elvis found one of the round, colored ornaments and batted it under the tree, then shot beneath and disappeared from view.

Matt smiled while Krystal rolled her eyes. "I think he's more excited about this tree than I am" she said, but she was smiling.

Matt rested his hand against her cheek and smiled down at her. "So, you still on for tonight?" he asked.

"I was never off" she replied and stood on her toes to kiss him. "What time?" she asked.

"As soon as you're ready. I was going to take you to Johnny's so you don't have to get all dressed up. You look beautiful anyway" he replied.

Krystal's cheeks flushed as she smiled up at him. "I'm ready, just wait one minute" she said and hurried upstairs to freshen up her make-up and dab on some perfume. Johnny's was her favorite restaurant in Aspen Valley and the most popular since it was the only steakhouse.

After running a brush through her hair, Krystal hurried back downstairs and took Matt's outstretched hand.

Country music poured from the speakers and could be heard over the loud chatter. The walls were decorated with country and Native American décor.

As usual, the bar was packed as well as the wood dance floor where several couples went through several steps of line dancing. Krystal wondered if she could get Matt on the floor. She was relieved when the waitress seated them at a table that was right by the floor.

"Would you like to dance?" Krystal asked just as Matt picked up his menu. He looked at her with a smile. "We just sat down" he said. She shrugged.

"So?"

Matt laughed, "let's order first, then we'll give it a try" he said reaching across the table and squeezing her hand. Krystal smiled, then picked up her own menu even though she already knew what she wanted.

Across the room, Derek sat with his new friend, Cody, and Cody's wife, Ellen. Ellen had brought along her best friend, Amy, who was also single and now, Derek found himself being hooked up with a woman he didn't even know.

Both Ellen and Amy had dressed the cowgirl part and wore open, button up, long sleeved, plaid shirts with white tank tops underneath, snug jeans, cowboy boots, and a cowboy hat.

Both women were also trying to get their dates to go dance with them on the dance floor.

"Maybe when a slow song comes up. You know I can't dance like that, Ellie" Cody said motioning towards the floor where the couples pivoted and did a quick thing with their feet.

Amy tugged at Derek's arm, "come on, Derek. Dance with me" she pleaded. He looked over at Cody and sent him a silent look which Cody just returned with a smile. "Maybe when Cody dances" Derek muttered.

Ellen and Amy pouted for about a minute before they put their heads together and disappeared into another one of their women conversations. Cody rolled his eyes, but he was smiling.

Derek looked around trying to keep his gaze from Amy. He was trying to be nice, but Amy had been such a surprise and Derek hadn't been prepared. Besides, she was the exact kind of girl he wasn't looking to date.

Sighing, he turned to look over the menu and prayed Amy and Ellen carried on their conversation throughout the rest of dinner.

"Will you dance with me now?" Krystal asked holding out her hand and smiling at Matt from across the table.

The waitress had just left with their orders and Krystal was itching to get out on the dance floor and refresh her line dancing.

"Do I have a choice?" Matt asked, but he was smiling as he took her hand and led her to the floor.

A slow song had started up as soon as they walked onto the wood. Smiling, Krystal rested her hand on Matt's shoulder while her other was taken by his. After he rested his hand on her waist, they began moving slowly.

Krystal didn't see Derek and Amy walk on because she had rested her head against Matt's shoulder and closed her eyes with a smile on her lips as Matt pulled her closer.

Derek froze when he recognized the couple dancing nearby. He had seen the man from somewhere, but he couldn't quite remember. The woman, though, he recognized instantly as Krystal and felt his heart sink at the sight of her with another man.

Amy wrapped her arms around his neck and pulled her close to him as she smiled up at him. Nearby, Cody and Ellen were lost in their own dancing.

"You have beautiful eyes, Derek" Amy said sweetly and dropped her eyes to his lips as she brought her face closer. He tried to pull his head back, but she was holding him so close to her. He tried to gently push her back a few inches and failed when she pressed herself against him. This woman had had way too much alcohol already. He could smell it on her breath and felt his stomach twist uneasily.

His eyes drew back to Krystal and thought he'd lose it right there. Her eyes were closed and a small dreamy smile was on her lips. The man who held her was resting his head on top of hers and had the same dreamy look on his face.

The vet. That's who he was. Dr. Sheperd.

He closed his eyes and turned away when he felt as if someone had punched him in the stomach. No wonder she had turned down his offer to have lunch, she was seeing someone else.

Amy's eyes widened when Derek moved her back more firmly, then her brow furrowed in anger as she pushed him back. She stormed off the floor without saying a word.

Cody and Ellen noticed and watched as Amy

waved goodbye, then stormed out of the restaurant. Both sent Derek an apologetic glance and nodded when he motioned that he was going back to the table.

As soon as the song ended, Matt and Krystal walked back to their table just as the waitress brought their salads.

Throughout the rest of dinner, they looked across at each other with a look of love struck teenagers.

"So what happened with Amy?" Cody asked as the three of them started eating. The restaurant had become more packed within the last half hour and was filled with loud chatter that Cody almost had to yell over.

"She was moving way too fast for me" Derek replied and looked up at Ellen, "sorry, I feel bad with her being your best friend" he added. She waved his apology off and smiled, "don't worry about it, Derek. Amy can be a little ..um .. crazy when she's had a glass of any alcohol."

"How're the kids?" Derek asked her and watched as her face lit with pride.

"Jake hit a home run and the winning point at his last Little League game. Oh, we're having his birthday party this weekend and you're invited" she said.

"How old is he now?"

"He'll be eight. He's growing up too fast. So is

Emily. She's my youngest and she'll be six in a few months. She's playing soccer now" Ellen said and smiled warmly at Cody, then turned back to Derek.

"Why haven't you found someone, Derek? You're such a sweet guy. When I first met you, I was so surprised to learn that you didn't have some gorgeous woman at home waiting for you."

Derek looked down at his plate, "I guess I just haven't found the right one yet" he replied and smiled when Ellen snorted, "yeah, that's what you all say. I was the one who put the first moves on Cody. He was too shy to do anything" she said and kissed her husband on the cheek.

Derek thought about telling them that the girl he wanted to be with was sitting on the other side of the restaurant with another guy, but he didn't want them forcing him to bring up his past mistakes so he stayed quiet and kept eating.

A half an hour later, both Krystal and Matt walked towards the front of the restaurant hand in hand.

Derek's heart leaped in his chest when his eyes locked with Krystal's and the two stared at each other for a long time.

Finally, she offered a small, friendly smile, then followed Matt outside.

Derek turned to look at both his friends, who had suddenly stopped talking about their son's party, and blushed a little when he saw them looking towards the door that Krystal had just walked out of.

Cody and Ellen looked at each other with a knowing glance, then looked at Derek, who had lowered his head.

"Wow. Even Amy couldn't compete against that one" Ellen said with a smile.

Derek looked up to see the smiles on their faces, but the curious gleam in their eyes.

Sighing, he leaned back and told them about Krystal and about what he had done.

"Dude. It's been, what? Nine … ten years. Somewhere around there. You should be over her. It looks like she's over you" Cody said taking a bite of his prime rib.

Derek's eyes darkened, "I know I should be over her, but no matter how hard I try, whenever I see her, I … I can't."

Ellen leaned forward, "we'll help you. Amy may not have been what you were looking for. I have hundreds of single friends" she said with a smile.

Cody groaned, "she does. They all made moves on me before she did."

Derek laughed.

Chapter 15

Krystal was going over some charts the next morning when a small knock sounded on the door.

"Come in."

Emily opened the door and poked her head in.

"Dr. Jacobson. There's someone here looking to adopt the Tibetan Mastiff."

Krystal's head shot up as relief spread throughout her body.

For the past month, the Mastiff had been up for adoption through the clinic. Several people had come to see her, but none of them had wanted to take her home.

"Thank you, Emily" Krystal said and stood to follow the technician out to the waiting room.

She stopped when she walked into the empty waiting room and spotted Derek looking at some pictures and awards on the wall.

Emily took her seat behind the desk to answer a phone so Krystal took a minute to really look at Derek while he was distracted.

He still stood like a tall, thin seventeen year old with his shoulders hunched and his hands shoved deep in his pockets.

Today, he wore a loose black shirt with a skull on the front and Krystal had a sudden flashback of his Slipknot shirts.

She had taken one of them back when they were in love and had worn it every night to bed. She had never given it back.

He wore baggy black pants and sneakers which now carried dirt and grass stains.

His hair was the same style it had been when he broke up with her, but a little shorter.

Her eyes traveled down his body, then back up as she felt a tiny electric shock somewhere deep within her heart.

Derek could feel her. He had known she walked in the room as soon as the technician took a seat and answered the phone, but he hadn't turned around because he had felt her eyes on him.

They hadn't felt angry, just curious and he needed a minute himself before he turned and looked at the woman he was falling deeply in love with all over again.

Krystal shook her head to clear the memories as she cleared her throat.

"Hey, Derek. What can I do for you?" she asked taking a step forward as he turned around.

He wanted to pull her against him and beg her to forgive him. He wanted to see the love in her eyes whenever she looked at him instead of seeing her cool stare.

Taking a deep breath he walked forward, keeping his hands in his pockets so his mind didn't make his body do something foolish.

"I've been thinking and I would really like to adopt that dog. My house will be done soon and I would like to have a companion when I move in" he said stopping in front of her.

He felt too close.

Krystal wanted to lift a hand to his chest and press him back, but she kept her hands at her sides and looked up at him.

The smell of his cologne drifted to her nostrils and made her heart hammer against her ribs. It was the exact same scent he had worn years ago.

Forcing a smile, she stepped back, "alright. Come with me" she said and led him towards the kennels.

Awkward silence passed between them as she led him down several halls, all deserted and silent.

"You guys aren't very busy today" Derek said quietly and felt his heart jolt when their elbows brushed.

Krystal tried to hide the flush that came to her cheeks, "yeah, it should pick up by noon" she replied.

The kennel grew noisy with excited barks and pleading whines when Krystal led Derek through the door.

She walked over to the kennel where the dog sat patiently and took her leash off the hook.

"I'll bring her out so you can see her" Krystal said.

Derek watched with a small smile as Krystal slipped into the cage and knelt by the big dog. She had always been good with animals. Even ones who didn't know her.

As she clipped the leash to the dog's chain collar, stroked her head, and whispered something to her, he found himself taking a trip down memory lane.

It had been the second time she was over at his house just a few weeks before their senior year was due to start.

They had swum in his pool almost all day. Derek could remember how good she looked in a bathing suit and had felt his heart fill with love when she swam into his arms.

Later, when they had gone back inside, she had begun stroking his two cats. Normally, the cats weren't friendly, especially to strangers, but their backs had arched under her fingers and purrs had escaped their throats. His dogs had really liked her too.

The sound of the gate opening snapped Derek from his memory.

The big dog was sitting in front of him looking up with large golden eyes.

Her coat had been recently washed and brushed

and her nails had been clipped.

"We haven't exactly given her a name, but most of the handlers have been calling her Maggie. I guess she reminded one of them of their old dog, who was named Maggie" Krystal said with a shrug and laid a hand on the dog's head.

Derek hesitated, then knelt in front of the dog.

For a while, the two just stared at each other, unsure of what to do.

Just when Krystal was about to move the dog back, her tail wagged and her tongue flicked out towards Derek's outstretched hand.

Letting out a quiet sigh of relief, Krystal handed the leash to Derek and watched as he began stroking her head and neck.

"If you want, you can lead her around and get to know her a little more. When you're ready, I'll be inside" Krystal said and was took a step back.

She turned.

"Wait."

Derek's voice stopped her and made her turn back around to look at him with raised eyebrows.

"Would you be able to walk with us?" he asked.

A warning flashed in the back of Krystal's mind and she hesitated for a minute.

"Um. I have charts I have to go over before patients start coming in and …"

Derek was waiting patiently, but Krystal could see the hope in his eyes.

"Just for a little bit" she said quietly and led the way to the door that would take them outside.

Krystal and Derek walked in silence with the dog between them as Krystal led the way towards a trail that she enjoyed walking when she needed to clear her head.

She knew it wasn't a good idea to go into the woods with Derek alone. He was already stirring feelings inside her and she considered him dangerous at the moment, but she also knew it would be easy to keep him at a safe distance after she had done just that for the past nine years.

"I come out here whenever I need to clear my head. It's a good way to relax after a stressful day" she said as her body began relaxing.

Derek turned to look at her and felt his heart fill with love at the relaxed look on her face and the small smile on her lips. He had to look away when the memory of kissing her popped in his head.

"It sure seems like a good place to relax" he agreed and watched a bunny disappear into the brush.

Maggie's ears pricked in interest, but she remained at Derek's side.

"You guys did really well training her" he said reaching down to stroke the dog's head.

Krystal smiled, "thanks. It took forever before I finally got her to learn some manners. There were times I just wanted to give up."

"You were never the giving up kind, Krystal" Derek said stopping and looking at her.

The two of them stared at each other for a while before Krystal took a deep breath and started walking quickly without saying anything.

Derek hurried after her. "So … I saw you with Dr. Sheperd last night. Was it business or a date?" he asked. She didn't need to answer, he already knew it had been a date and one of many.

Krystal stopped and turned, "what are you doing here, Derek?" she asked. Derek heard the pain in her voice.

"I came to adopt Maggie and I wanted to talk to you" Derek said. "I haven't seen you in so many years and I just wanted to catch up and start over."

Krystal shook her head and continued walking, but she remained silent as she shoved her hands in the pockets of her lab coat.

Today, she wore colorful scrubs with paw prints and white tennis shoes.

"Yes, I'm seeing Matt now. I have been for the past month. We have a lot in common and we really like each other" she said, then closed her mouth before she told him anything else.

Derek remained silent as he digested her words.

"Krystal…" he said quietly and was surprised when she stopped and whipped around.

He could see tears shining in her eyes along with pain and anger.

"When you're ready, bring Maggie back to the clinic and I'll have Emily go over the papers with you. Good day, Derek" she said, then walked briskly away. He considered going after her, but he didn't.

Instead, he turned and continued down the trail.

Krystal hurried into her office and closed the door behind her. She wished she would've said goodbye to Maggie, but she just couldn't face Derek again. Not when he was bringing back the memories, the pain, and the anger that she had worked so hard to bury and forget.

Taking a deep breath, she moved back to her desk and opened the chart she had abandoned.

When her door opened, she tensed thinking it was Derek, then relaxed as soon as she realized it was Matt.

He could tell something was wrong. That was the reason why she just rushed into his arms and pressed her cheek to his chest as he held her close to him and ran his hands up and down her back.

Matt had recognized that look in her eyes. It was the same look she had had whenever that Derek guy came around and tried to talk to her.

He closed his own eyes. Derek was clearly trying to fix things between him and Krystal. It was clear to Matt that Derek still loved her, but he wouldn't give her up that easily.

Once Krystal was relaxed and back to working on the chart, Matt walked into the waiting room where Derek was signing the adoption papers.

For a brief second, the two men looked at each other and in that brief second, silent warnings were passed.

Krystal sat back and rubbed her temples with

her fingers. It was past six, which meant everyone had left the clinic for the night, and she was finally done going over the charts.

She couldn't stop thinking about what had happened between her and Derek earlier that day. Nothing had really happened, but Krystal had seen something in his eyes which had made her knees go weak.

He wanted to talk to her and she was being a coward. Running away whenever she started to feel something for him.

Sighing, she closed her eyes. Maybe they should talk, but somewhere when she didn't have a thousand other things on her mind.

Opening her eyes, Krystal grabbed her purse and car keys and started to walk from the office when Matt walked in.

"You leaving?" he asked and she nodded.

"Oh, I was going to see if you wanted to watch a movie and order some pizza tonight?" he suggested.

Krystal's heart dropped. "I'm sorry, Matt. I'd really love to, but I'm beat and I think it would just be best if I went home and got some sleep" she said.

She could see the disappointment, but there was also an understanding. "Sure. Okay, I'll see you tomorrow then" Matt said with a smile and bent to kiss her goodbye.

"Okay."

Krystal couldn't sleep. She laid in bed and stared at the ceiling. So many things were going through her head that she didn't think she'd ever get to sleep.

Sighing, she tossed back the covers and shivered slightly as she stuck her feet in her slippers and reached for her robe.

A cup of hot apple cider would help her sleep and warm her cold body.

As she stood at her sink looking out the window with the warm mug in her hands, Krystal couldn't get what had happened earlier that day out of her mind.

She remembered a time when she would've done anything to have Derek look at her the way he had that day. Even to just have him acknowledge her presence instead of making her feel unwanted and invisible.

Krystal took a sip and sighed as the hot liquid warmed her insides.

What was she going to do? She couldn't let herself be hurt by Derek again, but that didn't mean she couldn't talk to him and be friends with him again. She couldn't be hurt like that again if they were just friends.

Feeling her eyelids grow heavy, Krystal downed the rest of the hot apple cider, washed out her mug, then headed back to her room with Elvis at her heels.

Chapter 16

Derek jumped when a cold wet nose was practically shoved into his ear and turned to look at Maggie.

She had sat on her haunches and was looking at him with her tongue hanging out.

"Don't tell me you have to go again" Derek muttered and groaned again when he saw that it was only four in the morning.

Dragging himself out of bed, Derek followed Maggie into the kitchen and opened the slider door so she could go out and do her business.

He shivered in the cold night air despite his baggy sweat pants and white t-shirt and closed the door until Maggie was finished. A minute later, she scratched at the glass.

"Now go to sleep will you. Thank you" Derek said when Maggie jogged over to the dog bed in the corner and laid down. Everything that had been the dog's in Krystal's apartment had come with her so Derek didn't have to go out and buy new stuff.

"Please, don't drink any more water and just let me sleep" he said and headed back to his room. He considered closing his bedroom door, but if Maggie needed to go again during the night and couldn't get to him, he'd have a disgusting gift waiting for him when he finally did wake up.

Derek dropped onto his bed and pulled his sheets over him. He was out as soon as his head touched the pillow.

Derek woke at seven-thirty the next morning and yawned as he stretched his arms over his head.

The sun was casting a dark golden light across his room and he had to shield his eyes before they could adjust.

This had been the first time, since Derek had moved back to Aspen, that he had finally been able to sleep in. That didn't mean he didn't get the day off. He had a thousand things planned for that day, which included cleaning up Maggie's mess in the small backyard and decorating his small apartment with Christmas decorations.

Derek had never cared for coffee so instead, he heated some water and grabbed a packet of hot chocolate mix.

Maggie was stretched out on her side and snoring loudly when he walked into the living room. He smiled as he plopped down on the couch and laughed when she jumped as soon as the TV turned on.

The weatherman was talking about the snow that had started falling in the middle of the night and how some of the roads were being closed. For all the kids in town, the weatherman announced a snow day. That was when Derek finally noticed how white it was outside.

How could he clean up dog poop when he couldn't even see it?

Derek turned off the TV and walked over to his window to look out and took a sip of his hot chocolate.

He could remember those rare days back in high school when they were given a snow day. Snow days in Aspen were rare since they got snow every winter and everyone, including bus drivers, were used to driving on the slick roads.

He remembered the first snow day he shared with Krystal.

Both had been excited to learn they were able to go back to sleep instead of getting up and going to school and when they had finally emerged around ten, they had been excited about playing in the snow with their fellow classmates.

With Aspen being so small, everyone lived near each other and the main meadow where they usually hung out or played sports was only a few blocks away.

Derek had met Krystal there and even now he could feel his heart hammer at the memory of the way she had looked that day.

She had been wearing one of his old hooded sweatshirts under a bulky, white, winter coat with brown fur around the hood, jeans, and snow boots. A beanie with their school's logo and colors had been covering her head and her blonde hair had spilled out from under it to frame her face.

It had been long and wavy then.

Her eyes had been bright in excitement and her cheeks and nose had been pink from the cold. Gloves covered both her hands so her fingers didn't freeze.

She had laughed at him because he came out wearing only a hooded sweatshirt, jeans, and sneakers while everyone else had been bundled up in winter wear.

For a long time, the two of them competed in snow ball fights against their fellow classmates. It had been girls against the boys.

Derek closed his eyes and smiled as he remembered.

He had been chasing Krystal with a snow ball in his hand and listening to her constant giggling as she tried to run as fast as she could through the ankle deep snow.

They had disappeared into the woods surrounding the meadow and a few times, Derek had lost sight of her because she had run behind some trees.

He remembered the cold shock as one of her snowballs hit him in the back of the head, then slid down into his sweatshirt.

He had whipped around to see her standing behind him with a flirtatious smile on her face, her arm back, and her fingers wrapped around another snow ball.

It was then when the ice from the snowball slid down his back and made him howl and hop around trying to get the snowball out of his sweatshirt.

Krystal had dropped the snowball she was about to throw at him and sank to the snow in a fit of laughter.

Derek finally got the snow out and bent over to roll some snow in his hands to form a perfect ball.

Krystal was laughing so hard she didn't see what he was doing and screamed when the snowball hit her beanie.

She had stopped laughing and raised her eyes to meet his, then scrambled to her feet and ran towards him with her arms stretched out.

He hadn't run. He had stood there with a smile on his face as she plowed into him with a giggle and sent them both to the freezing wet snow.

In a fit of giggles, they had rolled a few times before coming to a stop with him hovering over her.

He had looked down into her beautiful hazel eyes. The giggles had stopped as a warm smile spread across Krystal's lovely face. That was when Derek realized he was deeply in love with her.

Resting his hand against her cheek, he had lowered his head to press his lips to hers. She had wrapped her arms around him and kissed him back, then pulled back to look up at him.

"Can I get up now. I'm getting soaked" she had whispered.

Derek had immediately helped her up and wrapped his arms around her as they walked back towards the meadow.

"I love you" he whispered.

Krystal stopped in her tracks and turned to stare at him with wide eyes. He had been scared she would run because it had been the first time he ever told her, but instead, she smiled again before throwing her arms around his neck.

"I love you too, Derek."

Derek sighed as he opened his eyes to look out at the snow again. It took him a minute to register just what he was looking at, then his heart plunged in his chest before coming back to hammer against his ribs.

Why was she here?

That's all Krystal could think as she stood outside Derek's apartment and stared at the front door. His was the only one that didn't have a wreath.

She wanted to turn and flee, but her shoes felt as if they had become frozen to the grass.

Krystal shook her head and started to take a step back when the front door opened and Derek stood looking out at her.

Why did he have to bring back everything she had worked so hard to forget?

"Krystal. What are you doing here? It's early" Derek said and waved her over, "come in, come in. It's cold out here."

Krystal didn't want to, but she found herself walking forward and into Derek's apartment.

Maggie scrambled to her feet and with an excited bark hurried over to Krystal and head butted Krystal's hand.

Thankful for the distraction, Krystal knelt in front of the dog and stroked her head.

"If it's too early, I can come back later. I was going to anyway. I have some work I have to do at the clinic and I thought I'd stop by before, but…" Krystal said as she stood and shook her head. She sounded like an idiot and she was embarrassing herself.

"It isn't too early, Krystal. I'm awake. It's not like you woke me up" Derek said and offered her a warm smile.

Just then, he noticed she was dressed nicely and looking exactly like the teenager he had just been daydreaming about and he was still in his t-shirt and sweat pants.

"Hold on. I'm going to go throw on some clothes. Make yourself at home" Derek said and hurried to his bedroom leaving Krystal standing in the living room trying to decide what she should do.

Maggie whined and nudged Krystal's hand again so Krystal sat down on the couch and lost herself in her thoughts as she stroked the dog's soft fur.

Upstairs, Derek paced in his room trying to gather his own thoughts together. He finally grabbed one of his black t-shirts and pants and dressed before taking a deep breath and heading back downstairs.

Krystal stood when she heard him come in and turned to face him. Her stomach twisted when she realized just how incredibly handsome he had become.

"I should come back later. I'm sure you have a lot to do and I have stuff I need to finish," she said.

Derek stuffed his hands in his pockets; "you know, you don't really have to leave. I have time to talk" he said quietly and took a step towards her. Krystal took a step back as she felt her cheeks flush.

"No. I need to go. I really do have a lot I have to catch up on," she said quietly as Derek walked closer.

"Do you really, Krystal. Or are you just trying to run from something?" Derek asked quietly and saw Krystal's cheeks flush again, this time in anger. "I really do have things to do. I don't know why I even came here. It was a mistake. I'm sorry I wasted your time" she said and started for the door.

Derek grabbed her arm when she passed him and turned her around to face him. Her skin tingled where his hand held her firmly, but gently and her knees grew weak under his gaze. She was really close to his face and that made her both nervous and excited.

"Why don't I come pick you up when you're finished and we'll go to dinner just as friends. I really do want to catch up on things, Krystal" he said quietly.

For a while, they looked into each other's eyes, then Derek's gaze dropped to her lips. Something flashed across his face before he gently moved her away.

"I'd like that" Krystal heard herself say quietly.

Only You

"Why am I so nervous? I shouldn't be nervous" Krystal said in an irritated voice as she brushed her hair in the bathroom, later that afternoon. She had showered and changed about a hundred times, then re-applied her make-up and grew frustrated about what she should do with her hair.

All day she had been thinking about this date and looking forward to it, but now she was nervous and dreading it.

"It's not a date. He is just a friend" she told her reflection firmly. With a heavy sigh, she dropped her chin into her palm and stared at herself in the mirror.

Matt had been a little uncomfortable when Krystal told him about her plans for that night, but he had night shift at the clinic and hadn't been able to do anything with her anyway to change her plans with Derek.

"As long as you two are only friends. I have to say, I'm not comfortable with you being with another guy" Matt had said.

Krystal had heard the jealousy and had given him a big kiss, "I promise nothing will happen. It's just to catch up on things and start things over as friends. Just friends" she had assured him.

"It couldn't be done in public or over the phone?" Matt asked. Krystal had sighed quietly. It could have been done that way, but she felt better if she was somewhere without distractions.

"Matt. Don't worry, okay. Trust me."

Matt had still been uncomfortable, but he trusted

Krystal. Still, he knew he would need to keep himself busy so he didn't think about her having dinner with another guy.

Krystal straightened when the doorbell sounded. Taking a deep breath, she looked herself over one last time, grabbed her purse, then headed to the door.

She was relieved and a little disappointed to see that Derek hadn't brought any flowers or chocolate with him like he had done on their first official date. That told her that all he wanted was to be friends. She just couldn't understand why that bothered her.

The silence between them on the drive to Chili's wasn't awkward, it was comfortable and that helped Krystal to relax.

When they were seated, Krystal reached for a menu. She already knew what she wanted, she just needed to keep her hands busy and she wasn't ready to look Derek in the eye.

"I remember the last time I was in here. You were our waitress" Derek said looking around.

Krystal raised her eyes to meet his and felt her heart leap before she dropped them to her menu again.

"I remember that too. You were with some girl who gave me a look as if she thought I were some kind of competition" Krystal said and forced a smile.

Derek looked surprised for a minute, but the look vanished as he smiled.

Only You

"That was Ashley. She could sense something was going on between us that night. I assured her nothing was going on, but she must have seen right through me" he said and lowered his eyes back to his own menu.

Krystal was silent as she tried to come up with something else to say. She sighed in relief when the waitress arrived to take their orders.

"So. I hear you're building a house" Krystal said once the waitress walked away. Derek nodded as his eyes met hers.

"I'm hoping it'll be done early next year so I can move out of the apartment" he replied and laid his hands on the table.

"What about you? Are you going to stay in your apartment or are you planning on moving into a house?" Derek asked leaning forward a bit.

Krystal caught a whiff of his cologne and lost her train of thought for a minute.

"Um… I'm hoping to get my own place once I have the money. I also want to start my own clinic at home curing all animals. I have all the plans figured out in my head, I just need to get started" Krystal said and took a sip of her root beer.

Derek smiled. "I knew you'd always follow your dreams, Krystal, and I know you'll have one of the best clinics once you have it running" he said quietly.

Krystal shifted uneasily as she offered a weak smile.

"What are you planning on doing?" she asked,

"or what do you do? I know you had to get the money you used to build that house from somewhere."

Derek leaned back. "I took over my dad's metal shop when he retired. All the work he was doing for the shop and for the Coast Guard put him back in the hospital. He had to have back surgery and once he got out of the hospital, my mom and I were able to convince him to retire and let me take over. Somehow I was able to make it one of the best and moved up to welding."

"Oh. I'm sorry about your dad, but I'm happy about how well your business is running. I remember how it was starting to get hard to run" Krystal said and Derek nodded.

His eyes lowered, then raised again.

"About that, Krystal. I'm sorry I took all my troubles out on you. I know how much I hurt you" he said quietly.

Krystal tensed as a chill ran down her spine.

"Don't, Derek."

Derek leaned forward and covered her hand with his before Krystal could pull it away.

"No. I feel horrible about what I did to you. I didn't want to realize just what I was doing to you" he said.

Because his hand on hers was sending unwanted feelings throughout her body, Krystal pulled it away.

"No, Derek. You don't know just what you did to me" she whispered and was relieved when their dinner arrived.

Derek didn't bring the subject up again even though he wanted to get rid of all the tension that passed between them. He knew it would be better to talk to her privately about that subject instead of bringing it up in public.

He felt himself relax when he saw that Krystal had relaxed as he talked about how his family was doing and even got her to tell him about Brian and Amanda's wedding.

When Derek led Krystal from the restaurant later that night, he felt everything had gone just the way he hoped it would.

Chapter 17

Krystal couldn't help but think about her "date" with Derek as she jotted down some notes in one of her patient's charts.

She had called Matt as soon as Derek left to assure him that nothing had happened. He had sounded extremely relieved to know that she was home and that Derek hadn't tried anything.

He would never admit it to Krystal, but he had been pacing around the clinic and in his apartment all night wondering what was going on and thinking seriously about going to the restaurant to keep an eye on Derek.

He hadn't though. That would just tell Krystal that he didn't trust her and he didn't want her thinking that.

Still, he couldn't fight the unease that was forming in his chest and hoped that Derek would stay away from Krystal now.

As he stood in the doorway and watch Krystal jot down notes, Matt could tell she had something on her mind. He always knew when she was off in another world by the crease in her brow.

"Taking a side trip, Dr. Jacobson?" he asked in

a teasing voice.

Krystal jumped and turned. It took a minute before a smile spread across her face.

"Hey, Dr. Sheperd. How's that kitten you had to operate on this morning?" she asked.

"He's drugged, but he'll live" Matt said and closed the door before walking over and kissing her quickly and gently.

"How are you?" he asked smiling down at her.

"I'm fine. A little drowsy, but fine. I get to work on my first horse today so I'm excited" she replied and felt her heart rate quicken at the thought of working on her first large animal.

"I heard. Congratulations" Matt said with a smile.

He had been the one to recommend Krystal to the horse owner and was interested to see how she handled the large animal on her own.

"Thank you" Krystal whispered and kissed him once more before hurrying out to call in her next patient.

The big, dapple gray gelding snorted and tried to shy away when Krystal stuck the needle into his neck.

Her assistant handler tightened his hold on the lead shank while the owner stood back and watched as Krystal injected the liquid into the horse's vein.

The gelding only needed his yearly shots, but he was making the whole visit more difficult.

Krystal patted his shoulder when she had finished with his last shot then nodded to her handler, who led the gelding back towards the trailer while the owner pulled out her check book and jotted down the amount Krystal gave her.

"Thank you so much, Dr. Jacobson. I have to admit I was a little uneasy when Dr. Sheperd told me he wouldn't be able to give Jasper his shots, but that he had a new vet whom he highly recommended. I can be very protective of my Jasper. He's all I have left, really" she said and Krystal nodded in understanding.

"Now, after watching you, I'm glad he recommended you" Ms. Montgomery said and handed Krystal the check.

Krystal thanked the woman, watched as she left the barn and drove away with her gelding in tow, then headed back to the main clinic.

A few weeks later, Krystal sat in Aspen Valley's only real estate office across from her agent who was explaining the forms that lay on the desk in front of Krystal.

She had finally earned enough money to buy herself a house that she had been eyeing ever since high school. It was a coincidence that the house was up for sale now that Krystal had enough money.

Krystal remembered how excited she had been to learn that she had enough money in her account to buy a small house without going into debt, and how she had been even more excited to find the house that she had always called "her house", in the paper and listed in Krystal's price range.

She had called the agent of the house, Michelle Gray - who happened to be someone she knew back in high school - and had asked to see the inside.

Just walking through the front door had been enough. Now Krystal was signing all the paperwork that needed to be signed and handing Michelle the wad of cash she had pulled from the bank.

"Congratulations, Krystal. You can move in as soon as you're ready" Michelle said with a smile as she handed Krystal the key to the front door.

"Thanks so much, Michelle" Krystal said and surprised Michelle by throwing her arms around her neck in a friendly hug.

Michelle had been one of the rich, preppies back in high school and hadn't been the nicest person or the most liked.

As soon as Krystal left the office, she dropped by the hardware store and bought several cardboard boxes before heading home to start packing. Her plan was to be moved into her new house before Christmas.

Her plan went perfectly. Just a week before Christmas day, Matt, two of his friends, and a few of Krystal's friends arrived to help her load boxes and furniture into the Uhaul truck.

Elvis grew disturbed by all the commotion so Krystal put him in her empty room until it was time to leave. She already had his carrier ready for him and had his food, bowls, and toys packed neatly in one of the boxes.

By the end of the day, all of Krystal's furniture and all of the boxes were moved into her new house. Matt stayed behind to help her unpack the more important things.

"Looks like this place needs some repairs" he said and Krystal nodded in agreement as she looked around. The former owners hadn't taken very good care of the house. The carpet was stained and stunk and the walls needed to be re-painted. There was also a leak in one of the corners and in one of the pipes under the sink.

"I'll just rip up the carpet and replace it with wood flooring" Krystal said. Someone else may have been dreading all the work that needed to be done, but Krystal was looking forward to making the house hers.

"I can repair all the leaks and major repairs" Matt suggested, "and if you want help with re-flooring and re-painting, I'd be happy to help" he added.

"I'd like that" Krystal told him and stood on her toes to kiss him.

He finished helping her unpack most of the boxes labeled KITCHEN, then took her out to dinner and a movie.

The next morning, Krystal took some money out of her bank account and went back to the hardware store to purchase paint.

Matt had given her the day off so she spent the

day moving her furniture away from the walls and laying down paper.

An hour later she stood wearing an old, close fitting, navy blue t-shirt, and paint splattered jeans. She had paint on her hands, arms, and her cheek and had her hair pulled up in a ponytail so it didn't get in her face.

She had her favorite, local country radio station on and sang along with Gretchen Wilson's "Redneck Woman" as she rolled bright blue paint on the half finished wall.

Elvis occasionally wandered over to sniff at the paint and a few times Krystal had to shoo him away before he stepped in the paint and walked all over the house.

The ringing of the doorbell broke through her music. Krystal turned and frowned when she saw that it was only noon. Matt was due over as soon as he finished work at the clinic to help her paint, then take her to dinner.

Setting her paint roller down, Krystal wiped her hands on her jeans and walked to the door.

When she opened it, she was surprised to see Derek standing on her front porch.

"Hi. I heard you had bought yourself a house and I wanted to come see if you needed any help with anything?" he asked with a smile.

The sight of her in paint splattered clothes and barefooted was driving him crazy, but he kept his smile friendly and his hands in his pockets.

Krystal smiled and stepped back to let him in.

The smell of fresh paint greeted him.

"I was just painting" Krystal said and eyed his clothes, "Matt's due over later to help, but I could use a hand now if you don't mind getting a little dirty."

Derek shrugged and walked towards the different colors of paint that were sitting on the floor.

Krystal watched as he knelt over and grabbed a paint roller and a tray, then straightened, turned, and smiled, "I'll start on this wall."

The air was light and friendly between the two of them as they talked and laughed over the music.

Krystal found herself relaxing as she rolled the paint roller up and down the wall.

"This is really a nice house" Derek said and looked outside, "and you have a lot of land."

Krystal nodded, "yeah, I was excited to learn that it sits on a good ten acres. It has a good sized master bedroom and two spacey bedrooms and good bathrooms. I was surprised when I saw what it was priced for, but I put the offer in quickly" she replied and rolled her sore shoulders as she examined what she had done. She still had a lot of work, but she was looking forward to finishing it all.

"I heard you were thinking of ripping the carpet up and putting down wood. I could do that for you with no charge if you want? I also know someone who can get you the flooring for a good price" Derek said turning his head and looking at her. She smiled at him, "thank you, Derek. I might just take you up on that offer if Matt ends up getting too busy. He already told me he'd do all the harder repairs for me."

Krystal saw Derek's face fall in disappointment, but a second later it was gone and he was smiling, "just let me know" he said and turned to keep painting.

The two settled in comfortable silence as they worked with only the sound of the radio drifting through the house.

Matt slowed when he saw the black car parked in Krystal's drive-way. He knew who it belonged to and felt a bubble of anger and jealousy forming in his chest.

Matt parked behind Krystal's car and climbed out, then stormed to the front door and walked in without knocking. If they were doing something, he wanted to catch them off guard.

Disappointment and relief washed over him when he realized they were on separate sides of the room painting. Both backs were turned to him and the house was silent except for the low tunes of the radio.

"Hey, Krys" he said and saw both startle and turn.

Something flashed in Derek's eyes before he turned to continue working, but a loving smile spread across Krystal's face as she lifted her arms to wrap them around his neck and pressed her lips to his.

"Hey, Matt. Um, Derek came by to see if I

needed any help so I told him I could use some help painting until you came over" she said.

Matt forced a smile, then his eyes traveled to Derek's back before turning back to hers. "That was nice of him, but I'm here now so I can take over."

He tried to keep it sounding friendly, but a look flashed in Krystal's eyes before she turned to look over at Derek whose hand had paused on the wall.

She could sense the competition between the men and rolled her eyes before turning back to Matt.

She didn't smile up at him or tell Derek to leave. Instead she stepped away from Matt and picked up another roller.

"I'd get done quicker if I had two people helping."

The air lost the lightness it had held when it had just been Derek and Krystal and was replaced with tension.

Krystal ignored it and continued working while trying to keep a light conversation and hoping the two men didn't start trying to impress her so she liked one more than the other.

Ever since she and Derek had had dinner, they had become close friends. He had called a few times when she had been lonely and needing someone to talk to. Now he was being a good friend in helping her with household chores. That's all he was being, a good friend. But Matt was acting as if Derek was trying to take his place.

Men, Krystal thought and smiled as she rolled her eyes.

At seven-thirty, Krystal dropped her roller and turned towards the kitchen, "I'm going to fix us something to eat. It's my way of thanking two handsome men for their wonderful help" she said and smirked knowing she had just caused another itch for Matt by calling Derek handsome.

Matt caught up with her in the kitchen and took her arm, "I thought we were going to dinner tonight" he said. Krystal smiled and kissed him on the cheek.

"We are. Kind of. I'm making you dinner, Dr. Sheperd. We're having dinner here" Krystal said and turned. "I meant just the two of us" Matt said in disappointment.

"Derek is my friend, Matt. I'm not going to kick him out and not give him any food when he's been so helpful today" she said.

Matt couldn't help but feel his jealousy take over, "I'm sure he's been helpful in more ways than just painting" he muttered and was surprised when Krystal spun around, her eyes flashed. He winced as if he expected to feel her hand connect with his cheek, but both her hands were balled in fists at her sides.

"How dare you, Matt. I never expected something like that to come from you" she said coolly and turned to busy her hands so they stopped shaking.

Anger had flared inside her at his words as well as hurt. She spun around again, not realizing she had a knife in her hands. Matt took a step back.

She finally noticed and put the knife down, "how could you say something like that, Matt. Do you not trust me?" she asked. This time her tone was sharper.

"I trust you, Krystal. I just don't trust Derek" Matt said feeling his own anger bubbling.

Krystal threw up her hands, "I can't believe you, Matt. This isn't like you. Derek is just a *friend*. How many times do I have to tell you?" she snapped.

This time she saw Matt's eyes flash, "Just a friend? Krystal, you and I both know how Derek feels about you and it is far more than friends. Unless you're blind, you can see it in his expression every time he looks at you" Matt snapped back.

"Get out, Matt. Just get out of my house" Krystal said. She was no longer yelling, but her voice was dangerously low. "See, you're letting him stay and making me leave" Matt said.

Krystal's face turned beet red, "GET OUT" she screamed and pushed him. Just then, Derek walked in.

"Are you okay, Krystal?" he asked.

Matt spun around.

It all happened so fast that neither Krystal or Derek had a chance to prepare themselves.

One minute, Matt's hand was raised, then swinging and the next, Derek was falling back into

Krystal's kitchen chairs.

Krystal jumped between Matt and Derek before Matt could do anything else and turned cold eyes to Matt.

"Get out. Get out, now" she said quietly.

Matt glared at her, then stormed from the house. At the door, he turned.

"It's over, Krystal" he yelled, his words echoing through the house and in Krystal's brain.

Krystal turned to Derek who was slowly getting to his feet and touching his already bruised and bleeding mouth.

"Oh, let me get you some ice for that, then I think you should go too, Derek" she whispered and turned to put some ice in a cloth, then handed it to him.

"Krystal…"

"No, Derek. Please go. I need to be alone" she said and weakly smiled as she laid a hand on his arm, "thank you for the help today" she said.

Derek smiled back and winced at the pain in his lip, "your welcome, Krystal. Call me if you need to talk" he said and walked from the house.

Krystal waited until he had driven away before she slid to the floor and pulled her knees to her chest. She rested her forehead against her knees and let the tears come.

Chapter 18

The next morning, Krystal dragged herself out of bed and into the bathroom to take a shower. She wasn't looking forward to going to work that day and having to face Matt.

It didn't help her mood very much when she stepped outside and was pushed back by the icy wind. Gritting her teeth, Krystal lowered her head as she closed the front door behind her, then sprinted for her car. This was a bad move on her part.

Just before she reached her car, her shoe landed on a patch of ice and the next thing she knew she was flat on her butt on the cold concrete with her eyes squeezed shut to keep the tears from falling.

Krystal got slowly to her feet and rubbed at her bruised tail bone as she unlocked her car and slid inside.

She shivered as she waited for her car to heat up and blew into her gloves hands to try and warm them.

The snow was falling heavily and the roads were slick with ice. Krystal drove slowly and felt her heart skip every time she felt her tires slide a little on a patch of black ice. These were the times she was grateful that Aspen Valley was such a small town.

Only when she was safely parked in her parking spot did Krystal let out the breath she had been holding, but as she carefully made her way towards the clinic doors, she felt her body tense up all over again. She would rather deal with icy roads than facing an angry and jealous man.

Krystal opened the door and felt the warmth soak through her clothes and finally through her skin.

Several of the technicians and assistants were already there so the clinic was filled with talk and laughter. Krystal also noticed it had finally been decorated sometime over night.

Krystal lowered her eyes as she made her way to her office. Matt had probably done it when he got home from her house.

As she set her purse in the drawer of her desk, she couldn't help but understand why Matt had been angry and jealous. She had been spending a lot of time talking to Derek and she knew she'd feel just as angry if she showed up at Matt's looking forward to spending time with only him and finding another woman in his house.

She had to apologize.

Krystal couldn't find Matt anywhere so she headed back to the stairs that led to his apartment and slowly headed up. His door was closed and when she tried the knob, she found it was locked.

Krystal gently knocked on the door. "Matt, it's Krystal. I really need to talk to you. Please open the door?" she called gently and knocked again.

She stood and waited. After knocking several times and begging, Krystal took a step back and turned around. She had begged a man to come back to her once and all it had done was make things worse. She wouldn't be that stupid again.

The sound of the lock turning and the door opening caused Krystal to turn around. Emotions flooded through her as she came face to face with Matt.

She was surprised to see that he was still wearing plaid pajama pants and a gray t-shirt. "Matt, I'm soo sorry" she said and stepped forward.

Krystal expected him to tell her off or close the door in her face so when he opened his arms to her and enveloped her in a warm embrace, she was both surprised and relieved.

"I'm sorry, too, Krystal. I overreacted" he said and buried his face in her hair.

"No, you had every right to overreact" Krystal said pulling her head back so she could look up at him. "I promise I won't spend so much alone time with Derek anymore. I realized that I would've felt the same way you did if I came over to find an old woman friend in your house. I'm sorry" she said and pressed her lips to his. He held her closer and kissed her back.

All night, Matt had been tossing and turning. He had been beating himself up over telling her it was over between them and had been dreading facing her. He couldn't have handled it if she hated him. Matt had been up since five pacing his apartment and gulping down cup after cup of coffee. He hadn't even noticed the time until Krystal showed up.

Matt stepped back, but kept rubbing her arms with his hands, "I'm sorry, too. Uh, I'd better go get dressed. I didn't realize what time it was. I'll see you down there in a bit" he said and kissed her once more.

Krystal smiled in relief and gave him another long hug before she turned and headed back downstairs. The sound of barking from the waiting room never sounded so good to her.

To make up for the night before, Krystal took Matt out for an early dinner and when they got back to Krystal's, Matt helped her paint some more.

"If you want, I'll come over tomorrow to rip up the carpet and old floors. You were able to get the new flooring okay, right?" Matt asked and Krystal nodded with a smile, "yep, they should be delivering everything tomorrow morning so if you want to come over around noon, we'll get started on that" she replied. Matt nodded and gave her a quick kiss before turning back to the wall.

She wanted to get the walls and floor done before she started unpacking everything.

When Matt wasn't paying attention, Krystal found herself looking at him out of the corner of her eye with a small smile on her lips. She was falling in love with this man, but she was too shy to tell him.

A few days later, Krystal stood beside Matt with a smile on her face as she looked at the new gleaming wood floors. They had finally finished that afternoon.

"It looks so great, thank you" Krystal said and wrapped her arms tightly around Matt to give him a kiss. His lips curved into a smile against hers. "Your welcome, Krys" he said when she stepped back.

Krystal turned with a smile still on her lips. Now she could start unpacking all her boxes and rearranging her furniture. That could wait until the weekend.

Krystal grabbed Matt's hands, "I'm going to get cleaned up, then I'm taking you to dinner to thank you for all the help you've given me this past week" Krystal said and backed towards the stairs. "Well. Then I'm going to head home to clean up too. I'll be back around seven to pick you up" he said and tugged Krystal forward for one final kiss before he left.

Chapter 19

Krystal sighed heavily as she stared out the kitchen window at the rain and snow. The roads were all slush, but she knew they'd be ice within a few hours. There was no way Matt could drive in this weather.

Cupping her chin in her palm with her elbow resting on the counter, Krystal tried to think of something to do. Her small portable radio she kept in the kitchen was playing one of her favorite love songs.

Krystal jumped and gasped when a bolt of lightning lit the darkening sky followed by a loud rumble of thunder. A second later, the power went out casting Krystal into darkness. What light was left outside made it easy for her to see around the house once her eyes adjusted so she walked towards the open box where she had put all her candles and pulled them out.

Within minutes, her house was lit by candlelight and a mixture of fragrances filled each room.

Krystal grabbed a box and frowned when she realized she hadn't marked this one. It was smaller than the others and lighter. Curious, Krystal carried it into the living room where she set it on the coffee table, then plopped down on the couch and pulled the box open.

She coughed at the dust that came off the top and with a furrowed brow, reached into the box and pulled out a thin, brown leather, photo album. Krystal felt her heart skip a beat when she recognized it. Beneath it were her other photo albums of her family and friends, but this one she had made specially for her and Derek when she was back in high school and in love with him. She must've packed it without realizing what it was when she moved out of the house after graduating. She had never really gone through her albums until now.

Krystal set it aside and reached in the box for the others as another crack of thunder echoed over her roof.

She thought of calling Matt, then remembered her phone was dead.

Sighing, Krystal opened the first and smiled as she fingered through the pages that were filled with her and her family. In each picture she was a little older. The last two pictures were of her in her cap and gown. In one, she was standing beside Jason and in the other, she was standing with her parents. She remembered that day. Jason had been the one to take the photo of her and her parents.

The next photo album was filled with pictures of her and her friends from high school and college. Not one was of her and Derek.

Her eyes drifted back to the smaller album. The

reason for that was because all the pictures that had Derek in them were in that one book. Krystal set the album, she had just been looking through, aside and reached for the small leather album.

As she flipped through the pages and looked down at her and Derek smiling up at her. They had been taken at school, formal dances, when they had gone out with friends, around Krystal's house and Derek's house, prom in their junior year, track meets, and ones of them together smiling or kissing for the camera, Krystal started having flashbacks. Something she hadn't had in years. She remembered how embarrassed Derek had been kissing her while someone took a picture. Afterwards they had laughed about it and he had kissed her more passionately afterwards. Krystal squeezed her eyes shut and let the memories swarm her...

"Hey, Krystal. Come meet some of the guys" Chase called and pulled Krystal into the game room. There were several guys sitting on the sofas and all of them held an Xbox controller in their hand. Their eyes were glued to the screen and occasionally one of them cursed when their opponent delivered an attack which left them dead and one point closer to their game being over.

Krystal had recognized the game as Halo 2 and had smiled when she realized how into the game the guys were. She'd be lucky if they even glanced her way.

"Derek, I'm going to kick your...."

"Hey, guys. This is Krystal Jacobson. Remember the girl I told you about?" Chase called interrupting the foul remark.

Krystal beamed. Chase had talked about her. It felt great to know that since she couldn't stop talking about him to her own friends. She had developed a huge crush on him and had been overexcited when he invited her over to his house for one of his friend get-togethers.

When she turned back to look at the guys she was surprised to see that every pair of eyes were locked on her instead of the screen where all four characters stood waiting for their player's next move.

She smiled weakly and felt her cheeks flush under the gaze of one particular set of golden brown eyes which were larger and more interested than any one else's.

"Hey. Um, you guys should keep playing before someone attacks you" she said. Just after she finished, the girl who was playing the fourth guy ran towards one of her opponents and attacked him.

That caught the attention of the guy with the golden brown eyes. He turned back to the screen when he felt his controller vibrate in his hands and cursed under his breath. He wasn't just cursing because he had been attacked and was getting close to dying, he was also cursing as he tried to figure out what kind of feelings were swarming through his body.

As soon as Krystal had entered the room with

Chase, he had felt something warm in his chest. Her scent had drifted to his nostrils, but he hadn't thought much of what he was feeling. Until he noticed everyone else had stopped playing and was staring at her.

He considered attacking all of them to save him a few lives, but his eyes were drawn to her and that's when he felt as if his heart had exploded.

Krystal gave a small wave even though the guys had turned back to the screen and followed Chase into the kitchen where all the snacks were sitting on tables.

She couldn't help but smile when she heard a chorus of "dang" coming from the game room and she knew it wasn't directed at the game.

The guy with the golden brown eyes was everywhere she was for the remainder of the night, but he never said anything to her. She soon learned that his name was Derek when Chase asked him a question and at one point she played a game of ping pong with him.

Later that night when she was about to leave, he asked her out. She could hear the tremor in his voice and had felt bad about her reply.

Krystal saw the disappointment creep into his eyes when she told him she had feelings for someone else, but when she looked deeper into his eyes, she too felt something warm inside her. Two weeks later, they were dating.

Krystal had never gotten a chance with Chase. A few days after his party, Chase asked another girl out so Derek and Krystal started talking more and more. The second time he asked her out, she had smiled and nodded.

From then on, the two were almost inseparable. Their relationship grew each and every time they were together and it was nice when they both joined track. Practice and meets gave them more time to spend together.

Before Krystal knew it, they were celebrating their year anniversary and exchanging kisses whenever they could. She had already told him she loved him several times and he had done the same. Everyone believed they'd be together forever, especially Krystal.

Then that day arrived, the one Krystal had been unconsciously dreading since the first day she and Derek started going out...

Krystal jumped when the sound of her doorbell echoed through the house.

She dropped the album in surprise and jumped a little at the sudden noise.

Krystal turned and frowned when she realized it was still really stormy out. Then she smiled. Maybe Matt had come over anyway.

Krystal got to her feet and started to walk across the room when she stopped and turned. If it was Matt, she didn't want him seeing that she had been looking at pictures of her and Derek.

She put the album back in the box, dropped the

box on the floor, then hurried to the front door.

"Derek" she said in surprise when she opened the door. He stood on her porch and gave her a weak smile. Krystal immediately stepped back and let him in.

"I'm sorry to drop in on you, but you know how I am with these storms and I needed someone to talk to" he said as he looked around her house. "Wow, you've gotten a lot done around here" he said. Krystal expected him to be disappointed that she hadn't asked for his help so when she didn't hear any, her shoulders relaxed only a little.

"Yeah. Now it's just unpacking" she replied and walked towards the kitchen, "I'll get some tea going. Make yourself at home" she said and waved towards the couches.

Derek crossed the room and plopped down on the couch. His eyes scanned the walls where pictures and Native American decoration now hung, then the floors where only a few rugs lay. Finally his eyes landed on the two large albums sitting on the coffee table.

"I really am sorry for showing up unannounced. I know Matt wouldn't like me being here without him around," Derek said. He could hear Krystal heating some water and pulling down mugs.

"He wouldn't and I kind of promised I wouldn't spend so much time alone with you because it makes him nervous, but I haven't seen you in a while. This one time should be okay" she called back.

Sara Myers

Derek smiled as he looked at her baby photos and the pictures of her missing a tooth. He started to open the second album, when the box caught his eye. Curiosity had him peeking inside to see if she had any more and his heart took a giant leap in his chest when he recognized the small leather album.

Derek reached inside and pulled it out. It suddenly felt light and warm in his arms as he stared down at it. He remembered the day Krystal had shown it to him and how they had playfully argued over who would get to keep it. She had won in the end and Derek had wondered what she did with it when he broke up with her a few days later. Something warmed inside him as he held it. She had kept it.

He remembered when she opened the door for him and he suddenly realized there had been something in her eyes. His eyes widened when he realized she had been looking through it just before he arrived and the look that had been in her eyes told him that all her old memories and feelings she had buried and hidden had come back.

"Do you still like sugar in your tea or…?" Krystal stopped in her tracks when she walked into the living room and saw Derek staring down at the little leather album.

He looked up to see her staring in horror and embarrassment and when her eyes met his, something passed between them. Something that they both had been forcing back for years and years each time their eyes had met.

Derek set the photo album down and stood. Krystal was still standing as still as a statue as he crossed to her and she remained standing motionless when he stopped and stood so close to her that she had to lift her head to look up at him.

Her eyes widened as his head lowered, but she stood still with her eyes locked on his as his lips lowered to hers. Her eyes closed and a groan escaped her when their lips met. Fireworks went off in Derek's brain as he wrapped his arms around her waist to hold her closer and felt her arms wrap around his neck.

Heat passed between them as Derek deepened the kiss and closed his own eyes as his hands rubbed up and down her back.

Suddenly, Krystal's eyes shot open. Placing both hands on his chest, she shoved him backwards.

Her eyes were huge and filled with love, horror, guilt, and anger. Her lips were now pursed and her cheeks were quickly reddening in anger.

"How dare you, Derek?" she cried and turned around, "I want you to leave, now."

He stepped forward, grabbed her arm, and spun her around so they came face to face again. That look of love that she had shown him so many years ago came and went in a flash, but Derek had seen it.

"I can't do that, Krystal. I don't want to and I know you really don't want that either" he said quietly. This time her eyes flashed.

"You don't tell me what I want. I want you out.

You're complicating things" she said and tried to pull her arm out of his grasp. He gently tightened it.

"I'm trying to fix things" he said and watched as Krystal shook her head.

"Yes, I am. I made a mistake, now I'm trying to fix it" he repeated firmly. Krystal closed her eyes, then opened them and glared, "kissing me when I have a boyfriend is not fixing things, Derek. Stuff like that just makes things worse" she snapped and tried to pull her arm away. "Let go of me, Derek."

"No. I won't do that Krystal. I did once and it was the biggest mistake of my life. I won't make that mistake again" Derek said quietly. Krystal went still under his hand.

"I moved on, Derek. I did what you told me to. It hurt like crazy, but I did because that's what you wanted. I loved you enough to let you go and accepted the fact that you didn't want anything to do with me anymore. Now you need to do the same" she replied, her voice shaking with emotion.

"I was never over you, Krystal. I tried to prove it to myself by pushing you away and that was wrong. I love you, Krystal. I've loved you all along" Derek said.

Krystal's eyes were shining with tears now. She was hurt, relieved, and angry.

"Well, I don't love you, Derek. Not anymore. I love, Matt" she said quietly and saw the pain flash in his eyes.

Derek gentled his hold on her arm and didn't object when she pulled her arm away and turned to stare out the window with her arms crossed under her breasts.

"You need to go, Derek. I'm sorry, but I just can't deal with this anymore. Maybe it's just best that we don't see or talk to each other anymore. I'm not going to ruin my relationship with Matt" she said without turning to look at him.

Derek felt frozen in place, but his head nodded slowly, "maybe that is for the best" he heard himself say painfully. "I'm sorry, Krystal" he said quietly and backed out of her kitchen, then turned and walked out the front door.

The sound of it closing echoed in her ears and her heart.

Chapter 20

"Would you stop worrying, they'll love you" Krystal said and kissed Matt's cheek as they stood outside her parent's house Christmas night.

Matt shoved his hands in his pockets and jingled his keys just as the door opened. Becky cried out happily and tugged her daughter and Matt into the toasty warm house before pulling them into a motherly embrace.

The smell of a cooking turkey filled the house and somewhere behind all the voices, Christmas tunes were playing.

Becky took their coats, "we have drinks in the kitchen so help yourself" she said and smiled up at Matt, "the men are outside. Krystal, go introduce Matt to your father" Becky said and shooed the two from the house.

Matt grabbed Krystal's hand as they stepped outside and all the men stopped talking and turned to study Matt.

"Guys, this is Matt."

At first the men were silent and staring as if they enjoyed watching Matt squirm uncomfortably under they gaze, then they smiled and welcomed Matt. Krystal smiled as she left them and headed back inside. She hadn't seen her mom in what seemed like ages and wanted to catch up on things.

"So, what's going on? I can tell something happened by just looking at you" Becky asked as she prepared the turkey. Krystal's eyes widened before she smiled and shook her head. Her mom never missed a thing and she knew it would just be useless to try to deny anything.

"A week ago, Derek dropped by and he kind of kissed me. I guess he thought he was trying to fix what he did wrong" Krystal said and watched her mom's eyes widen. Becky turned and stared at Krystal. "What did you do?" she asked.

"I pushed him away and told him that he wasn't fixing anything, he was making it worse. I told him to stay away from me" she replied.

What looked like relief passed over Becky's face quickly, then was gone as she stepped forward to look deeper into her daughter's eyes.

"You still love him, don't you? Even after everything he's put you through all those years?"

Krystal straightened as she turned her eyes away. Becky followed her gaze and smiled softly when she saw Matt laughing at something one of the guys had just said.

"You do, Krystal. You can turn away and deny it, but I know you. I know you're having a hard time right now because you're in love with two different men" Becky said and laid a hand on her daughter's arm.

"I honestly don't think Derek deserves to have you back. I'd rather see you with someone like Matt, but I also want you to be happy" Becky said and kissed her daughter's cheek just as the timer went off.

She left Krystal to sort through her thoughts as she pulled the turkey from the oven.

"You okay?" Matt asked later that night as he drove Krystal home. She snapped back to reality and turned to smile at him, "yeah, I'm okay."

Matt glanced at her and frowned. She was deep in thought and frowning slightly. He knew she wasn't okay. Something had happened and he was pretty sure he knew exactly who had been involved.

As soon as Krystal walked into her house, she closed and locked the front door before heading to her room to change into her warm pajamas and crawl under the covers.

Her head was pounding so she pulled her Tylenol down from her medicine cabinet in her bathroom and swallowed two.

Krystal was tired of thinking about Derek. He was supposed to be gone from her life, not taking it over again. She was with Matt now and she loved him.

As Krystal lay in bed, Elvis jumped up and curled up on the pillow by her head. He purred quietly as she stroked his fur and stared at the ceiling.

Only You

Within minutes, the Tylenol started to take effect and soon Krystal's mind was washed clean as her eyes slowly closed.

The next morning, she sat up straight and waited for her breathing and heart rate to slow as the dream faded. She couldn't remember much of it, but she knew it had been about both Derek and Matt.

Groaning, Krystal pulled her knees to her chest and wrapped her arms around them. After a minute of sitting like that and waiting for the remainder of the dream to fade, Krystal rubbed her face with her hands, then got out of bed and hurried towards the bathroom to take a hot shower and warm and soothe her aching body.

At the clinic, Krystal pushed Derek from her mind and focused completely on each of her patients that walked in.

Even though she hid her thoughts really well, Matt could tell she was troubled by watching her facial expressions when no one was around. Her hands kept running through her hair, which she had left down to hang around her face and shoulder, and her brow kept furrowing in confusion.

"Hey. How about we go out to dinner tonight?" Matt asked walking over and resting a hand on her shoulder, "it's clear you need to get out and do something to keep your mind off work."

Krystal raised her eyes to his and smiled weakly, "that sounds great. I could really use it" she replied and turned as she was called into one of the examination rooms.

Matt watched her leave, then sighed and shook his head. She wasn't acting like herself and he was growing extremely worried about her. Just then he saw Derek walk past the clinic and a bubble of anger formed in his chest.

Derek was probably just doing some shopping in the nearby stores. It wasn't like the clinic was the only building on the street. It was the fact that Derek hesitated and peered into the clinic with his hands deep in his pockets.

Through the glass, Derek's gaze locked with Matt's and for a long time the two men just stared at each other.

Matt's eyes turned from Derek when he heard Krystal walk back into the waiting room and waited to see if she noticed Derek standing outside.

She did.

Matt watched as she stared at Derek and clearly saw the emotions running through her eyes. His heart plummeted in his chest as he turned to look back outside to see Derek continuing down the walk. Something had happened between Krystal and Derek and Matt doubted it had been an argument.

"Dr. Sheperd, you have a phone call" Emily said interrupting Matt's thoughts and holding the phone towards him. "Thanks Emily, I'll take it in my office."

Only You

A whole month. How could Matt leave for an entire month? There was too much work that needed to be done at the clinic. Sighing, Matt placed the phone down and leaned back in his chair.

It had been one of his best friends, Danny Pasek, who was also a vet down in southern California, who had just called. Apparently one of the town vets had quit leaving Danny to do all the work. Now, Danny was begging for Matt's help while new vets were trained.

Matt sighed. There were enough people at the clinic in Aspen to keep things going while he was away, but he hated the thought of leaving Krystal when he was so worried about her.

Matt began rubbing his temples. Krystal would have more work piled on her with him leaving which would mean she would become more stressed. But then Danny needed him and there had been a time when Danny had dropped everything to help Matt get through rough times. Besides, Matt had already told Danny he would help. He hadn't even thought it through. The two had met in veterinary school and had become roommates and best friends.

"You wanted me" Krystal said when she walked into Matt's office. She frowned in confusion when she saw he was getting ready to leave.

Matt straightened and came around the desk to pull her into his arms. "I have to leave for a month. One of my best friends is having some problems and he needs help with his clinic and patients. There's currently someone being trained right now, but he won't be actually working for another month. I'm sorry, Krystal" Matt said and leaned down to kiss her.

"Don't worry about it, Matt. I understand your friend needs help and I think it's great that you're going to help him. I'll miss you like crazy though" she said and was surprised when she realized the last part was a lie. She would miss him, but a month away would give her some space to think things over instead of him constantly wondering what was wrong.

"I'll miss you too and I'll call whenever I can" Matt said and kissed her one last time before heading out the door to his car. His plane was scheduled to take off in an hour and a half and he still needed to pack for the trip.

Krystal watched him leave with her hands shoved deep in the pockets of her lab coat. She expected to feel a sense of loneliness as Matt drove away so she was surprised when she felt as if a weight had been lifted from her shoulders.

When Krystal left the clinic and headed towards her car, she realized she wasn't ready to go home. For a while she sat in her car while it warmed up trying to decide where to go. Finally she backed out of her parking spot and headed towards her parent's house.

"This is such a wonderful surprise. Come in, Krystal. Get in out of the cold" Becky said and stepped back so Krystal could walk into the house. It smelled like spaghetti and made Krystal's mouth water.

"Is everything, okay?" Becky asked as she headed back to the kitchen. Krystal followed her and helped her mom finish preparing the dinner. "Everything's fine. I think. Matt left for a small rural town down south this morning. He's helping his friend while another vet goes through training" Krystal replied as she stirred the spaghetti sauce.

Becky looked over at her daughter, "and is his leaving a good thing or a bad thing?"

Krystal glanced over her shoulder at her mom before turning back to stare into the sauce, "surprisingly it's a good thing. I feel bad, but it's like a weight has been lifted from my shoulders" Krystal said.

"Don't feel bad about that, Krys. Sometimes a woman needs her space to think" Becky said and finished washing the noodles before stepping beside her daughter.

Becky gently laid her hands on Krystal's shoulders and turned her around so they were facing each other, then looked deeply into Krystal's eyes.

Krystal turned her eyes away, but she knew her mom had already seen straight through her.

"You still love Derek, don't you?" Becky said quietly and smiled when Krystal's eyes snapped back to her. "I can see it, Krystal Anne Jacobson, so don't deny it" Becky said.

"You're still in love with Derek even after everything he's put you through. I can see that you forgive him, but you're still hurt. You want to go to him, but you're scared you'll be hurt again because you and I both know it'll hurt worse than the first time" Becky said and Krystal's eyes widened in surprise. Her mom should've been a psychic and Krystal told her so.

Becky laughed and shook her head, "no, I can't read other people, only my children. I can't even read your father sometimes" Becky said and looked away with a small, but loving smile on her face.

"You know, you're father hurt me once" Becky said so quietly that Krystal almost didn't hear her. Krystal's eyes widened, "what'd he do?" she asked.

Becky released Krystal's shoulders and turned back to the stove. For a minute, Krystal didn't think her mom would tell her, then Becky turned around again and took a deep breath.

"As you know, we became sweethearts when I was a foreign exchange student at our high school. God, the two of us were always together. When we weren't at school, we were out seeing a movie or out having dinner or over at each other's houses. I didn't want to go back to England. I honestly didn't want to go back to that princess lifestyle my parents had forced me to live for seventeen years. When I was here in the states, thousands of miles away from them, I was free to be a real teenager. I was free to go out with friends and not have to worry about a French or ballet lesson. The family I stayed with was wonderful. They were loving and weren't too strict and they had this wonderful three year old daughter. They became my family along with my other family back in England.

"Anyway, a few days before I was due to fly back to England, your father came over to say goodbye to me. I never expected the farewell he gave me. He told me we wouldn't work now that I was going back to England and that it would just be best if we went our separate ways and moved on. I was devastated. Then I saw him with another girl. I was on my way to the airport, but I wanted to find him and tell him how much I loved him. When I saw him walking with her down the sidewalk, she was hanging on him and the two of them were laughing. I felt as if someone had cut open my chest and ripped my heart from my body."

Krystal nodded in understanding when she remembered how she had felt the same way when Derek had left her.

"Your father saw me standing a few feet in front of him, my face completely pale. He stopped and the girl who was with him stopped and looked at him strangely, then followed her gaze to me. She turned out to be one of the good friends I had made so then I felt as if someone had punched me in the gut. The next thing I know, I'm running towards the limo my parent's hired to take me to the airport. I could hear your father running and calling after me, but I had gotten a head start and dove into the limo.

The driver closed the door and drove away. I didn't want to look back, but I did. Your father was standing in the middle of the street and for the first time since I met him, I could see tears running down his cheeks."

Becky paused as she pulled down plates and began setting the table.

"What happened then, mom?" Krystal asked as she set forks and spoons beside each of the three settings.

"I had already applied and been accepted to Aspen Valley University and despite what your father did to me, I wanted to go to college here in the states. It had been a dream of mine even before I met him. When I got home, I showed my parents the letter and begged them to send me to school in California. After a long time, they finally gave in and a few months later, I was back, but I was a completely different person. I made a lot of friends and dated, but never let things get serious because I couldn't stand the thought of being hurt again."

Becky paused and took a deep breath as a smile crept across her face, "then one day, I was walking with some friends down the sidewalk and I ran into Jeff. We were speechless as we stared at each other and when he touched my arm, it tingled. Everything I had felt for him came flooding back and before I knew it, he was begging me to forgive him. I yelled at him and said hurtful things. I've never been one to want revenge, but he had hurt me and I suddenly wanted to hurt him as much as he had hurt me. Next thing I know, his lips are pressed to mine, then I'm walking down the aisle in a white dress with him standing at the end beaming at me."

Becky sighed and turned back to the table as her words sank into Krystal's brain. "You took him back. Even after what he did to you because you loved him even though you didn't want to admit it" Krystal said with wide eyes.

Becky turned and dropped her eyes before raising them to meet Krystal's.

"Derek treated you as if you were everything to him when you two were together, then suddenly he's treating you as if you never meant anything to him. He didn't deserve to have you. He still doesn't."

Becky dropped her eyes again, "when you came to me Christmas night and I saw what was going on in your mind, I could only remember everything that happened between your father and I. I know exactly what you've gone through, but your decision is harder than mine was. I want to see you happy, Krystal."

Becky took Krystal's face in her hands and looked deeply into her eyes, "I want you to know that I really like Matt. I'd rather see you with someone like him, but I can also see how much you love Derek and it reminds me of how much I love your father even after what we went through. I can't make this decision for you. I just wanted to tell you that I understand exactly what you're going through with Derek."

Sara Myers

Krystal clutched her mom's hands in hers and looked back at her. Derek's seventeen year old face as he smiled down at her, popped into her mind and made her whole body heat. Krystal closed her eyes and let the old feelings swarm and take over her heart.

Chapter 21

A month later, Matt drove back into Aspen Valley and headed straight to Krystal's house. It was after six so he knew she'd be home relaxing after a busy day at the clinic.

Like her, he had done a lot of thinking over the past four weeks and even after trying to come up with a different way to fix things and failing, Matt had realized what he needed to do.

Krystal was in her kitchen washing the dishes when Matt's truck turned into her drive-way. Her heart started hammering against her ribs as she dried the dish in her hand and put it up in the cupboard before walking to the front door to let Matt in. She could tell he needed to tell her something as soon as he stepped inside.

"Let's sit in the living room" she said and led the way. Matt followed, sensing she had something to say to him as well. As soon as they sat, Krystal opened her mouth to speak, but Matt stopped her by holding up a hand.

"Krystal, I did a lot of thinking while I was away" he said and she smiled weakly, "so did I."

"Krystal. I've noticed how distracted you've been lately and for a long time, I just thought it was because of the holidays and all the patients we were getting. While I was away, I realized that what you were thinking about was Derek."

Krystal remained silent which surprised him. He had thought she'd try to defend herself and deny that. Taking a deep breath, he continued.

"I know how much you loved Derek, Krystal, and I know how much you still love him."

Here, Matt took her hands in his and kissed them while keeping his gaze on hers. "I love you, Krystal, but I know you'll always love Derek more no matter how much you deny it. I'll always care about you. That's why I have to let you go. I want you to know how hard this is for me to be telling you this, but I couldn't think of anything other than asking you to marry me."

He watched Krystal's eyes widen. Her expression wasn't in surprise or hope, it was in horror. Somewhere deep inside him, he felt pain at that. He shook his head, "but I can't do that and I won't." He squeezed her hands as he watched her try to hide the relief.

He leaned forward to kissed her quickly and gently. The spark that had been there once was gone. He sat back and smiled at her, "go back to Derek, Krystal. He's the one for you. You two were meant to be together" Matt said quietly and watched Krystal's eyes fill with tears as she leaned forward and wrapped her arms around his neck and gently press her lips to his, then held him close to her as she whispered in his ear.

"Thank you, Matt. I'll always love you."

He nudged her back a little so he could look into her eyes, "but not more than friends." She just smiled and nodded slowly.

"Then I'll always love you too."

Epilogue

Derek was standing in front of his new house when he heard a car pull down his drive-way. He turned to see who his visitor was and felt his heart skip several times in his chest when he recognized the sleek, silver car.

Krystal sat in the driver's seat wearing sunglasses and a heavy coat to keep out the frosty air.

The two of them stared at each other for a long time before Krystal finally emerged from her car and made her way over to him. He stayed where he was and just stared at her as she came to a stop in front of him. Only then did she remove her sunglasses so he could see her shining, hazel eyes. She wore no make-up, but she was just as beautiful to him.

He started to speak, but she held up her hand and motioned towards the house, "can we talk?" she asked. He nodded and led her inside.

"Do you want anything?" he asked and she shook her head. They walked into the spacious living room and sat down.

Maggie trotted in and laid her head on Krystal's knee. Silence settled for a long time before Krystal finally took a deep breath and raised her gaze to meet Derek's.

God, those eyes did things to her.

"Let me just start by telling you some things I've wanted to say for years" she said quietly and Derek winced.

Krystal dropped her head as her hands kept themselves busy by stroking Maggie's head and neck.

"You hurt me, Derek. You could've just gone and ripped my chest open and taken out my heart, then left me to die with how much you hurt me." Derek winced at the violent image.

"That wound took years to heal and even when it had scarred, it was still raw underneath. I cried for months and months even though you didn't deserve to be cried over. You deserved a good punch in the gut. I went through deep depression because of you. I just couldn't understand how you could be treating me as if I were everything one minute to treating me as if I were nothing the next" Krystal said repeating what her mom had told her.

"I tried to tell you I understood you needed your space and that I had finally realized just how much you had to deal with, but you wouldn't let me. I was dead to you and that broke something inside me. I didn't think I'd ever be able to love someone again. I ruined every relationship I was in after you because of you."

Krystal rubbed her face with her hands and gently pushed Maggie's nose away when the dog nudged her.

"I loved you even after the way you treated me and none of the guys I was with could even compare to you. I struggled to get over you and forget. I thought I finally did, but..."

She paused and fisted her hands in her lap as she raised her eyes to his, then got to her feet.

Derek just watched her as she crossed the room, took his face in her hands and lowered her mouth to his. It was a long kiss, one that was filled with passion and a mixture of love and anger. When Krystal finally pulled back, she could see herself in Derek's eyes. "God Derek, I've never gotten over you. I love you. I've loved you all along and I forgive you. That's what surprises me the most. I forgive you for what you did, but I'm scared that it'll happen again and that it'll just hurt twice as much. But then, I'm scared that I'll never be happy again if I can't be with you."

Derek brought his hands up and held her face in them as he looked down into her eyes. She looked back up and watched as he lowered his mouth to hers.

Her arms circled his neck to hold him close to her. He whispered her name, then deepened the kiss and pulled her closer as if he was afraid she would disappear.

Her hands lifted as she ran her fingers through his hair. Electricity was passing back and forth as Derek ran his hands up and down her back in a comforting and loving gesture.

"Give me another chance, Krystal. I love you. I

love you so much" he said when he broke the kiss.

Krystal looked up into his eyes. The love was back in them, but this time it was stronger. There was also a small amount of fear. In her mind she saw them as two seventeen year olds again who were madly in love with each other and felt her heart overflow with love.

Derek looked down at her now with hope and love on his face.

"Hold onto me, Derek. Hold onto me and never let me go."

Derek's heart exploded with love as he took her face in his hands and pressed his lips to hers.

"Never again."

Printed in the United States
117189LV00001B/64-111/P